PRAISE FOR

Eleanor, or, The Rejection of the Progress of Love

"Philosophically exhaustive yet profoundly human, this book sets itself the task of asking the big questions—What am I? What was I? What will I be?—in a style that evokes Lispector and Camus but with the self-referential and weary globalism of the current milieu. A consummately accomplished novel. A worthy treatise on the now."
—*Kirkus*, **starred review**

"Anna Moschovakis has done something remarkable."
—*Los Angeles Review of Books*

"Moschovakis's novel is braided and experimental, yet it looks for illumination in the plainspoken and the authentic."
—*The Wall Street Journal*

"*Eleanor* is a witty novel, studded with provocative literary and philosophical references." **—BBC**

"A novel about noticing and ruminating rather than assessing and concluding. The daily weather, interchanges with passing acquaintances, views out the window, are accorded the same attentive courtesy as love and pain. Life isn't seen as a grand arc but as one thing after another, second by second. The book offers each moment, each sentence equitably and leaves us to decide what is important and how." —*Star Tribune*

"Funny, intelligent, and sensual, although also unsettled, *Eleanor* is engaging from the onset and a welcoming new female voice."

—*Library Journal*

"By turns funny, melancholic, and provocative, Anna's novel undoes and remakes the conventions of realist fiction through repetition and compression of time. . . . It is 'luminously ordinary' in its progression, where profound shifts are as small as a postcard written or a hand touched."

—*BOMB*

"Moschovakis is in search of a way of presenting a woman's life that is not expressed solely through family and bonds with others—that rebuffs inherited conventions while acknowledging that women are still labouring their way through the mare's nest chaotically erected by patriarchy."

—*Frieze*

"Moschovakis has created a novel of great strength and flex. Much as it bends and twists and gyres, it does not break, in fact only accumulates more tensile strength from the motion, just as, one hopes, we all can do."

—*The Brooklyn Rail*

"Her prose is marvelously rich with meaning, conceptually dense and precise in phrasing."

—*Commonplace Review*

"[A] carefully controlled, intelligent novel of ideas."

—*Literary Hub*

"Performance art in print."

—*Publishers Weekly*

"A brilliant, visceral, sensual examination of the condition of being a woman, and the inherent struggles related to identity and authority that exist for all of us."

—*Nylon*

"[A] searching and poignant work that deftly positions itself between the unspeakable specificity of personal experience and the disturbing surplus of fungible narratives in our online world." —*Cleaver*

"Moschovakis' book seem[s] to arrange itself as we move, dream-like, through it, encountering a singular architecture of novel and novelist that challenges us to read and think towards new possibilities, new heights." —*Arkansas International*

"Moschovakis is a poet, and *Eleanor* is unmistakably a poet's novel, alert to the textures of experience but relaxed in the pursuit of plot." —*Lambda Literary*

"Moschovakis's characters are celebrations of the information-collecting prowess of women, of the way in which her characters 'weigh and consider' . . . an overwhelming amount of data throughout each day." —*Rain Taxi*

PARTICIPATION

PARTICIPATION

A Novel

Anna Moschovakis

COFFEE HOUSE PRESS
Minneapolis
2022

Coffee House Press books are available to the trade through our primary distributor, Consortium Book Sales & Distribution, cbsd.com or (800) 283-3572. For personal orders, catalogs, or other information, write to info@coffeehousepress.org.

Coffee House Press is a nonprofit literary publishing house. Support from private foundations, corporate giving programs, government programs, and generous individuals helps make the publication of our books possible. We gratefully acknowledge their support in detail in the back of this book.

LIBRARY OF CONGRESS CATALOGING-IN-PUBLICATION DATA

Names: Moschovakis, Anna, author.
Title: Participation : a novel / Anna Moschovakis.
Description: Minneapolis : Coffee House Press, 2022.
Identifiers: LCCN 2022016659 (print) | LCCN 2022016660 (ebook) |
    ISBN 9781566896573 (paperback) | ISBN 9781566896580 (epub)
Subjects: LCGFT: Novels.
Classification: LCC PS3613.O7787 P37 2022 (print) | LCC PS3613.O7787
    (ebook) | DDC 813/.6—dc23
LC record available at https://lccn.loc.gov/2022016659
LC ebook record available at https://lccn.loc.gov/2022016660

PRINTED IN THE UNITED STATES OF AMERICA

29 28 27 26 25 24 23 22   1 2 3 4 5 6 7 8

for Jo

The only pressing reason for changing a theory is disagreement with facts.

—Paul Feyerabend, *Against Method*

I can't position, I can't assure anyone of their ethical well-being.

Take this engine, the clerk says. You are living your electric life.

—Dionne Brand, *The Blue Clerk*

PARTICIPATION

ONE

TWO GROUPS

I never made it to Love, and now I hear it's defunct.

Anti-Love meets regularly, though attendance is spotty. At least I've done most of the readings.

Love, by contrast, will be a recuperation project.

Anti-Love is not, to be fair, billed as Anti-Love. It's billed variously as resistance, revolt, revolution. Sometimes it's billed (tentatively or defiantly) as Self-Love.

Love bills itself as itself, eponymous and proud.

Without the beginning of the story, it's enough to know that there is a drafty corner apartment, an all-night bodega out the window, a playground across from the bodega, quiet at night. There is an abundance of emotion—enough years, enough fucks and near-fucks and pseudo-fucks, enough expectations unanswered because unheard or unsaid—and it is that abundance that is known: a partial knowing, as excess is always, paradoxically, partial.

Without the beginning of the story, it is insufficient but still necessary to have a picture of the surround: not only the bodega and the playground, but the news reports filtering up from the apartment below. The news reports appearing at the top right of the screen, a stack of small explosions, almost registering, then, compulsively, swiped away.

There is a stack of books—on a coffee table, for example. An archive of future attention, or else a morgue.

Love isn't defunct, exactly. It's been reduced to a virtual form of itself. Flesh into type, an assembly turned list. I enter it, when I enter it, through a screen.

Don't be fooled by the present tense, the future tense, when they occur, which they will. This is a story about the past. It's already over.

When I say that the story is over, I mean that a merger has happened, which is not to say an acquisition. (This is a story about two groups.) I am also insisting on the safety of storytelling, to protect myself, and you, from a certain pain.

Story is a safe emergency.

One of the members of Anti-Love is a psychoanalyst, a fact rarely mentioned in our meetings, though the language of this fact—*safe emergency*—edges in. The psychoanalyst is from Buenos Aires, where an hour of therapy can cost the same as a burger; as a result, a large portion of the population is in treatment.

We absorb such unverifiable facts from conversation, and they become a part of us, they become us.

(Without the beginning, it is also necessary to have a picture of the second surround, some 150 miles away: a table in a room that is open to the public, dirty floor, a radiator that leaks. A village view out the window: gas station, neon lights, small mountain just behind.)

How are we to know who started things? At its peak there were ten of us in Anti-Love; we'd sit around the improvised wooden table, peer at one another over mugs of coffee or of beer. The idea for the group came from me, I've been told, though I remember it as always having been there. Not always, in the strict sense. It appeared when I needed it: an acquired taste. Tonight I met a man who was beautiful and tall, who wore capitalism like a well-fitting suit. Anti-Love recognized him, shone a light. For example.

Love was different. You wonder if I have a story to tell. I was invited to Love. The way salt is invited to the early-winter road.

I was invited and I said Yes, I said Send me the syllabus, I said I am only partially fluent in your language. I was told I was welcome nonetheless. Meanwhile, the neighbors were setting each other on fire. California was also burning—actually burning. The neighbors, aflame, sat on their stoops, extracting the burrowed tick of love from one another's skin.

It's everywhere in the news reports—swipe, swipe.

You don't have to believe me, but you can.

FACTS

I can't know what you believe.

I can offer you parable after parable, tale after tale.

I can tell you the one about Porous and Anemone, who came together over a shared sense of the word *expectation*. Anemone wanted things from Porous: a lack of friction mostly, but also small noises, an elbow extended into its vulnerability. Porous wanted everything to be decided (elbow in the ribs, far in). One day in the vestibule of one of their apartments, Porous had a change of opinion, which is not the same as a change of heart. The story ends there, with Porous leaking predictable tears, Anemone predictably backing out the door.

There is a theory of the psyche that claims *life narratives* are necessary to the formation of a coherent subjective self.

This theory has always terrified me. Maybe I'm afraid of stories. Or of selves.

Or maybe I confuse *coherence* with *cohesion*. The psychoanalyst once explained the danger of this mistake, of letting the left brain suppress what the right brain knows. The way we rush to make sense of things, invent airtight accounts, stories that *follow*. We depend on these unprovoked lies.

A *cohesive* story, the analyst clarified, may well lead to a desired result (we may get wrong why the bird crashed into the window, but the decals we put up save the next bird's life).

When I was a child, I thought swooping sparrows were hunters, hoping to nest in my unkempt hair.

But *coherence* doesn't come so easily, or have such immediate results. At this point in the analyst's explanation, I began to disappear. My eyes and ears wandered, to a fly buzzing in a spiderweb strung between the radiator and the wall. A session of Anti-Love had just ended; the winter sun had dropped behind the mountain and the gas pumps; the street was empty and I was spent. I struggled to understand the challenge I felt: if *cohesion* was marked by false order, by a completionism that held chaotic truths at bay, then *coherence* (its corrective?) consisted of work I didn't know how to do. What I recall about the distinction between cohesion and coherence is a feeling of desirous terror—or terrified desire—at the prospect of abandoning my attachment to the first before being able even to conceptualize the second.

What can be told, without inciting this terror? What kinds of stories, what narratives, invented or not?

Or are these the questions I'm training myself not to ask?

When dawn lifts itself over the corner apartment, the bodega glows. The playground waits for its portion of light. Late risers don't know this, but there is always a moment, sometimes fleeting, when the clouds brim pink. In bed, angled toward uncurtained windows, I wait for it. When there are no clouds, the pink separates itself onto puddles, passersby.

I can't know what has become me, what becomes.

Stack of unverifiable facts, archive of mistakes.

Some strays can attach to anyone, over and over.

WORK

This month, while work has stopped through no fault of my own, while I need to conserve what little funds I have (while I have *more time than money*), I will try to catch up; I will follow the syllabus of Love. I like to follow, but the syllabus has so many holes. In the beginning, I won't try to plug them. I can't make promises for the future—this being one of my failings, both in and out of love.

When I say work has stopped, I mean one-third of my work has stopped. I have three jobs, in two places, connected by a train. (I'm using the word *place* where before I used *surround*, though now neither term feels right.)

In one place, I work part-time in a café-bar that serves coffee, pie, and cheap wine in carafes. I like the job because the café-bar is slow and I can read; it's so slow I wonder how the owner, whom I never see, covers the bills. I wonder if, after paying me and the other part-time worker, he breaks even.

I've done the math, and the money I earn at the café-bar just covers the expense of commuting to the other place (surround) to fulfill the obligations of my other two jobs: the expense of the train, some food and drink, and rent for the time-shared room in the corner apartment with the bodega/playground view. The job at the café-bar helps me *break even*.

I could just call the two places *the village* and *the city*, since that's what they technically are.

My second job is different. My second job is as a mediator-in-training. When I get a call, I travel south to the city to assist my mentor with cases.

I can't tell you about the cases; they're covered by a confidentiality agreement I signed when I began my training, and which I sign again in front of each new set of clients. What I can tell you is that, to my mind, the work with my mentor is worth the hours I put in at the café-bar to support my commute. For one thing, the work is interesting; for another, it is the closest I have come to *investing in my future:* even at the apprentice stage, it pays the most of my three jobs.

But in the place where I am most often—in the village, where my life is manageable and where I work at the café-bar—it's hard to come by employment as a mediator. Though sometimes working at the café-bar feels like supplemental training.

My third job, the one at which I met the capitalist, is a holdover from my former line of work. It's a waged job, like the café-bar, but in the *information* sector rather than the *service* sector.

I don't like my third job. I have arguments with its purpose. I would like, once my current obligations to the capitalist are complete, to cut back to just the two jobs. I have only one mouth to feed, after all.

Unfortunately, the work that has stopped through no fault of my own is not the third job, the one I argue with and want to leave behind. My mentor has vanished and isn't returning my calls.

Now I have two jobs, but they aren't the two jobs I want. Still, a hole in my schedule has created the opening necessary to catch up with Love.

A SYLLABUS

I've fallen twice for philosophers. The first one studied a fascist—still does. The second one studied, still studies, forms of love.

The *Stanford Encyclopedia of Philosophy* sets out in classic triangulation:
 —Love as Union
 —Love as Valuing
 —Love as Robust Concern
 I recognize, from my Western philosophical *formation*, the triad of eros, agape, philia. I absorbed it as lust, altruism, friendship, often wondering in the intervening years how much damage that taxonomy, trivialized by time and lack of attention, has done.

The first philosopher and I never recovered from a betrayal. I succeeded, with the second, in transforming eros into philia, or finding the philia in eros—prying it out, over time. I sent him the syllabus to Love and he sent it back from his university post, annotated and marked. Love, stained already by Authority, History, Trust.
 I messaged the list:
 "Loves, I still haven't met all of you in person, and I regret the demise of the IRL sessions. I did share the syllabus with my love philosopher, as requested. Annotations forthcoming. Yours, E."
 This missive earned a single black heart from S, one of the members of Love I'd never met. I jolted when I saw their heart, then I liked it back.

We are not post-gender, but when it comes to names and pronouns—this decision predated my invitation to the group—Love tends toward the least binding. (This was explained to me as an experiment, a gesture.) On the list we are capital letters; we are all they/them.

Picture this against a backdrop of shift, a ground of categorical pause. Picture the clients: a husband and a wife, for instance. Their marriage has ended, something new has taken its place, within (provisionally, at least) the same walls. He walks around the house smiling for the first time in years. She retreats to her corner, begins the process of cleaning up and clearing out. They sleep separately, better than well. They put their arms around each other several times a day. Sometimes, for no reason but because they want to, they fuck.

(Is the story of the husband and the wife mine to tell? Does it preserve confidentiality to replace names with roles, details with abstractions? Does reducing it to gestures honor the contract, or break it?)

I jolted at S's heart "for no reason." Does it follow that I jolted *because I wanted to*?

The style of mediation I'm learning, have been learning, depends on the ability of the mediator to draw out unspoken needs from each party, to go beyond the surface narrative ("the conflict") to find out what the right brain knows. The phrase used in the Manual is *the story beneath the story*.

You could say the mediator shares some traits with the therapist. According to the Argentine analyst, therapeutic treatment depends on love being present—if not mutual then at least unidirectional, from therapist to client. This love, the analyst admits, can take effort. And isn't always possible to achieve.

Learning to draw out the stories beneath the stories told by my mentor's clients takes effort, especially when a reaction of confusion or defensiveness is sparked within me. When confusion or defensiveness becomes apparent in my body, my task is to reorient toward the client's story while taking note of the subject or dynamic that provoked me, on which I clearly still have *work to do*.

It's only now that I'm not actively being called to the field of mediation that I'm most actively reflecting on that field, viewing it with the peculiar, intimate distance of the cartographer. (And viewing that cartographic distance with the suspicion of the skeptic.)

I don't know if attention to this task of self-aware reorientation—if the labor it requires—falls under the category of agape. It may be just as important to eros and philia, or it may belong to a category of love still unnamed, or one named somewhere I have yet to encounter.

This category must be represented in Love's syllabus by its holes.

ANOTHER SYLLABUS

The last time Anti-Love met, we were down to three.

It was brutally cold; the streets were ice. The three of us sat around the big rectangular table, frequently rising to put the kettle back on or to extract a beer from the fridge.

The reading, which was from 1980, was about the politics of consensual sadomasochism in consciously anti-patriarchal love. Around our table, imbalances of experience were revealed, then modulated. I said "according to my friends" and "theoretically." I said "Don't you think the expulsion of 'the natural' from the erotic is the very definition of freedom?" My face grew warm, an embarrassment due less to an act of disclosure than to the desire to explain.

It occurs to me I could clarify that Anti-Love meets at the café-bar where I work—after hours, which isn't late, since we close at seven. Sometimes I forget what you know.

I miss my mentor, and I miss the mediation sessions. The style of training I received, am receiving—in principle, if my mentor hasn't permanently disappeared—is nontraditional, an attempt to redress assumptions that have historically plagued the field: assumptions of neutrality, of objectivity of terms, assumptions that all people have equal access to their ability to tell, fluently in the language of the mediation and without fear of retribution, their story. Let alone the story beneath it.

Sometimes the worst retribution is internal; this is among the hidden threats I'm being trained to see.

It occurs to me that the syllabus for Anti-Love was designed in part to redress assumptions that are analogous to those present in the old style of mediation, which the new style is attempting to correct. Problematic assumptions that may be all too present, that may linger (and this is part of our story, if you can call this a story) in the syllabus of Love.

One aspect of the new mediation technique is that even the attempt to create a shared narrative is intentionally, through the prolonged separation of parties during the interview stage, delayed. Of course, what the parties do on their own time—as with the husband and the wife, for example—is up to them.

It occurs to me that the games of dominance and submission that were at issue around Anti-Love's makeshift table might be framed in a similar way: as an example of biding—while a conflict is slowly, exhaustively excavated—one's time.

SUBSTITUTIONS

I'm supposed to be reading about love, but instead I keep reading about drugs.

The kinds of drugs I'm reading about fall into the category *psychedelic,* a category that—like notions of *truth, honesty,* and *fidelity* in thinking about love—is both more dull in its meaning and less clear in its relevance than people think.

Psychedelic ("mind-manifesting") tells us nothing about the nature of the particular episode of manifestation, or the dynamics of power (for example) that may have led to its occurrence. Just as truth, honesty, etc., tell us nothing about love's possibilities while telling us everything, though dully, about its corporate lie.

S strikes me—judging by their contributions to the list—as a person who would have a non-dull understanding of both love and drugs. As for the capitalist, I can't tell.

Did I mention the capitalist has an accent, that uncanny accent I once heard described as English of the Global Elite?

When I said I have three jobs (counting the one that has, perhaps only temporarily, disappeared), that was an oversimplification, a wish. I have tall piles of tasks—paid, unpaid, underpaid—at every moment. Some tasks are stragglers, old obligations, much overdue. I finished one of them yesterday; it involved the accidental rediscovery of another philosopher of love, better known as an anarchist of Science, or anti-Science. This rediscovery led me further off the syllabus.

I considered writing to S to suggest adding the anarchist to the Love readings. Does S know of the anarchist already? Does the capitalist? The capitalist may: he's an internationalist and an intellectual (and must of course, I remind myself, also be other things: parent, swinger, jock). I recall that among the members of Love is a bitterly anti-academic academic, and while I am not an academic, the anarchist philosopher is, or was.

Though he, too, must of course have been other things as well.

I resist writing to S. I am trying to learn to wait.

Meanwhile, the husband and the wife are still sleeping separately, are still putting their arms around each other often and fucking when they want. I assume this based on what I know, which is to say on extrapolation from what I have been told. I assume, too, a time limit to their experiment: each of them senses it but doesn't want to admit it to the other. They may be caught in the same form as were Porous and Anemone, their definitions mismatched, futurity meters out of sync.

It's too bad, I think, when I think of them. The form is not of their design. The anarchist would say, did in fact say, "We never know all the virtues that might give content to our lives, we have just started thinking on these matters and so any eternal principle we may want to defend today will most likely be overruled tomorrow."

He also said, or wrote, that "a life without mystery is barren and that some things, for example our friends, should be loved rather than understood."

This may also go for husbands and wives, or for other pairs and groups of people entering into relations of intimacy based, either positively or negatively, on that of husband and wife.

Or it may not. This is among the underlying subjects of both Love and Anti-Love.

The anarchist's formulation about love without understanding calls to mind the stack of books on the coffee table (archive, morgue). I pick one up—Pascal's *Pensées* in English translation, bought for a dollar months ago and unopened until now, though it's not the first copy I've possessed, not the first time I've opened it and read.

My memory for books is bad; when I try to recall them, it's as if whole passages and themes have been swiped away. Not just passages and themes. Let me give you an example.

The first paragraphs of *Pensées* propose a distinction between intuitive thinkers and mathematical thinkers. Between thought supported obliquely by common observation and thought supported directly by rarefied fact. I follow this distinction; I am a delighted reader. Entering Pascal's numbered paragraphs, my delight is bodily, a flood of recognition: he is speaking to me!

But the second paragraph speaks of men, makes clear that it speaks only of men, and I am not a man. This revision, too, I feel in my body, as an assault. He is not speaking to me! A small sword—swipe, swipe.

The paragraphs, at the outset, nearly alternate: to me—not to me—to me again! Swipe. Swipe. Swipe.

Of course, even the paragraphs I read as being addressed to me are not, in fact, addressed to me. But I learned long ago how, in the absence of explicit reminders of my ineligibility, to contort myself to gain entry where I wanted, when I could. This is a metaphor borrowed from the psychoanalyst, the way creatures under threat will rearrange their bodies to minimize pain.

Minimizing pain must be distinct from maximizing pleasure, but when it comes to reading for identification—for recognition—there can seem to be no air between them. In the best cases, when you read something, you feel like you've known it forever. In the best cases, you feel like it read you first.

The first time I read *Pensées*—or any number of books, of stories, countless examples come to mind—I understood the fact of this small sword of exclusion; I felt it, and yet I wanted, still, to love.

I imagine this scene and its aftermath: love swipes at the sword of exclusion with its bare hand, bleeds, scars over. Partial recall, its attendant insecurity and doubt, is the aftermath. Partial recall: the difference left when recognition is subtracted from love.

Remember this when, soon, we ask the capitalist about the peak-end rule. Remember how I calculated this difference for you.

⸏

When I say that I wanted to love—Pascal, or other books on the originary stack—I mean that I wanted, that I needed, to be *addressed.* And I was outside the field of address.

When I say that the swiping away of the sword results in a scar, I mean there is a numbness that arrives on the scene. Researchers at the intersection of psychoanalysis and brain science have documented the damage that occurs to children who are not sufficiently, routinely addressed. A blurring occurs that is dysregulating, that is dangerous.

Once this damage is located squarely in the past, the scar itself can be measured, tended to. The lingering blur is less frightening to look at, but is also harder to understand.

The blur may offer a way to think about *having a bad memory.*

We know it from our everywhere screens, how a swipe leaves a smudge.

MORE SUBSTITUTIONS

I can't stop thinking about S.

Instead of writing to them, per se, I email an excerpt of my notes about the husband and the wife, with cameos from the capitalist, the anarchist, and the rest.

I have no expectation that S will write me back, but I find that I am having thoughts about them, and that the thoughts are, categorically speaking, more erotic than filial. I find that there is something very specific about having erotic thoughts concerning a person whose appearance is so wholly unknown to me, who is without, among other things, a communicated gender.

I find that under the circumstances, certain body parts are easier to picture than others: the lips, the soles of the feet, the asshole, the shadowy region behind the ear. These become, when I think about S, the primary erogenous zones.

Sometimes, inadvertently, the image of these parts—the ones I have glimpsed, i.e., the first and last in my little list—on the body of the capitalist substitute themselves in for the mystery parts of S. In the back of my mind, I know I will see the capitalist again: at a scheduled meeting for work, at a series of scheduled meetings that runs no risk—unlike the Love sessions—of being suddenly discontinued. (This raises the question, of course, of the relation between availability and desire.)

Meanwhile, my mentor is still on the run. On the run, on the lam—my mentor is a mystery. I wonder if I have been sufficiently trained to continue our sessions with the clients, without supervision. There is an imbalance of access: I have the clients' contact information, but they don't have mine.

Should I call the wayward daughter and her harried single dad? Should I email the husband and the wife?

I am not sure who I should be, who I am. I have never found it easy to be clear about my role. I stare at the clients' information on my phone's bright screen.

My phone rings. The second worker at the café-bar is out with the flu. I put on my coat.

"Did you know that Ethel Kennedy was administered LSD therapeutically, and that when it was outlawed by the newly formed FDA in '66, Bobby protested its suppression and defended its life-altering potential?"

I was sitting on a friend's couch with the friend's partner, Pablo, talking about drugs. (The timeline's blurry, this wasn't long ago.) Soon the conversation turned to Pablo's relationship with my friend.

"Duration and frequency," Pablo offered, "are all there is, really, to measure. Why do we need definitions, labels, 'primacy'? Shouldn't comparatively large doses of duration and frequency be enough?"

Something had been troubling me, in the back of my mind, which moved to the front of it as a result of the question Pablo posed. The troubling thing is an old story, possibly the oldest (embarrassing to admit—in the same way that trying to get at something true about the erotic was embarrassing, last time Anti-Love met). It's a question about the nature of reality, and whether it can be shared. The part that had been troubling me was the way this question intersects with the practice of mediation, the way it intersects, even, with the definition of the term.

I once met a mathematician at a party who told me her field was intuitionism. I couldn't understand what little explanation she attempted to offer that night, over the music (Prince) and the wine (boxed). When I looked up the term, later, I found this:

"Intuitionism is based on the idea that mathematics is a creation of the mind. The truth of a mathematical statement can only be conceived via a mental construction that proves it to be true, *and the communication between mathematicians only serves as a means to create the same mental process in different minds."*

Emphasis mine.

୨

Now that I am able to observe my own (limited) practice of mediation from the compromised vantage of the cartographer, I can begin to wonder about the outsize role description plays in the process. All of the labor, all of the back-and-forth between parties, is successful only to the extent that the parties can agree about how their feelings, and how their relation, should be *described*.

Even in the best-case outcomes—again, my sample is small, six or seven cases, but varied—the relation itself rarely changes (enemies don't become friends, or ex-partners reunite). The feelings don't change, either, though sometimes they soften.

What changes is that in place of two divergent, conflicting realities, an extended process of triangulation has produced a single description about which—no matter how much regret and pain it contains—both parties can agree.

The same mental process, created in different minds.

What Bobby Kennedy actually said, in the senate subcommittee hearings on LSD, was, "I think we have given too much emphasis and so much attention to the fact that it can be dangerous and that it can hurt an individual who uses it . . . that perhaps to some extent we have lost sight of the fact that it can be very, very helpful in our society if used properly."

While Pablo and I were talking, about drugs and about love and then about the anarchist philosopher of science and so on, we left the space of another person between us on the couch, as if reserving the space—though it was cold in the room and we are both inclined toward touch—for my absent friend. This despite very low levels of duration and frequency between Pablo and me.

The night after my conversation with Pablo, I received an email from the capitalist.

It was not addressed solely to me: it was a work email, planning for the upcoming series of events that I had been recruited to cohost. The capitalist has a breezy way of communicating, as if his global citizenship came with a magic coat of belonging.

In Anti-Love, several sessions ago, we talked about *internalization* and *regulation*. It occurred to me, as the terms *Q & A format, tech needs,* and *learning outcomes* passed across my screen, that I had a growing desire to seduce the capitalist, to extract every ounce of pleasure he contained, then throw him out.

⚗

In a message to S, I described how aware I have become, when writing, of my tendency simply to name the people I'm reading, a tendency I tried to explain through the value (both the false and coercive value and the real, true value) *in these times* of drawing attention to the things outside of oneself that one likes or finds important. I signed off: "Sometimes I think of writing as just pointing."

I am not exactly a writer, mind you. Sometimes I try to write.

I typed the message on my phone from behind the bar the day I'd been called in to work unexpectedly. It was the third I had written to S without receiving a reply; it might, I figured, be the last.

I didn't worry I would be taken for a stalker. I worried I would be taken, by someone who wasn't inclined or ready to address me, for who I am.

As I hit Send, the door opened, letting in a blast of cold air: Margaret, who walked up and down Main Street every afternoon from five to five thirty, an aluminum cane in one hand and a handful of braided pleather bracelets in the other.

"You wanna buy one?" she asked, as always, her voice a soft, high, syrupy thing. I held up my left wrist, as always, to show the two that I wear there, stacked. "No more room on my arm!" I said—as always—and handed a can of raspberry seltzer over the counter, invited Margaret to sit, received a wave and an "O.K., thanks, bye!" in reply—and she was gone.

So I point: Winnicott (D. W., on mothering); Lorde (on anger); Sedgwick (on love); Klein, post-Klein; Ahmed (on being a problem); Delaney (on desire); Brand (D., on theory); Berlant (on optimism); Butler (O., also J.); James (W., on reality); Laplanche (on aggression); Winnicott (Clare, the wife).

Sometimes I ask a question while I'm pointing. For example: "How can eros and philia and agape gather together in a world that is characterized by fantasy but also, necessarily, shared?" A friend heard Moten speak for hours and, when I asked about it, paused: "He said *gather*."

How can anyone gather in a world that is characterized by fantasy but also shared?

I discovered Clare Winnicott only by accident while looking up her husband. She has a page on Wikipedia, a few paragraphs long. It tells me that "besides publishing some sixteen articles in her own right, she worked with, inspired, married, and edited the writings of D. W. Winnicott." It tells me that one of her articles is titled "Children Who Cannot Play."

"Worked with, inspired, married, and edited," I read aloud, attempting with my tongue to push the terms apart.

It's strange to miss people you don't deserve to miss. My mentor and I weren't close, though the training provokes a certain kind of intimacy. I have no right to miss S, a stranger.

What I know but can't see through the blur is that my sense of *what I deserve* needs undoing. That I have exactly as much a right to be addressed as does anyone, as do you.

TAXONOMIES

It's zero degrees today. Actually, it's New Year's Day.

I don't have a good track record with holidays: birthdays, anniversaries. You can ask the two philosophers, or any of the rest. I have, you might say, a fucked-up relationship to the expectations of others. The wife and I may share this trait; so may the anarchist, though he would use different words. Maybe you share it too.

It's zero degrees. A thin layer of ice has made a vignette of the window overlooking the bodega, itself vignetted by a string of holiday lights. A child the size of a fire hydrant stands next to a fire hydrant, bundled ridiculously in fire-hydrant red.

Weeks pass. It's still cold. No word from my mentor; Love, too, has gone quiet. The wife and the husband have scheduled a "talk," which is to say that in my mind they are due for a talk. The sun is bright and bears down on the owner of the bodega as he carries out a stepladder, positions it in the center of the broad and dirty window, climbs it, and begins to bring down the string of unlit lights.

I order a manual for growing psilocybin mushrooms. I download two books from one syllabus: *A Lover's Discourse* and *All About Love.*

I check, periodically and futilely, for a message from S.

On the radio, I hear a story about language, or about language games, though not Wittgenstein's. Instead, the old parlor game Twenty Questions.

According to the show's guest, in languages in which gender is not represented in the grammar—in which pronouns and nouns and adjectives are uninflected, shared by all—the game of Twenty Questions runs an unfamiliar course. Among speakers of these languages the question "Is it a man or a woman?" which often follows an affirmative reply to "Is it a person?" might not be asked until question nineteen or twenty, if at all.

Who is pictured while the other questions are being asked?

Pablo is a translator. An interpreter, actually. He explained to me, that night on the couch, how the movement toward inclusive usage in his language entails the transformation of each adjective and pronoun, through use of a new suffix or ending—an adjustment he contrasts to our targeted substitutions (such as "they" and "are"). I wasn't sure I liked Pablo, but he had things to teach me; this was clear from that evening and from others too. I liked my friend, very much, but she took off for a new life after discovering that the frequency and duration Pablo was ready to offer weren't enough.

Pablo is also gone now, but for different reasons. He is needed.

When I wrote about the bodega owner closing up shop, did you picture a person? How detailed was your picture? Did you make decisions, subconscious or not, about hair color, skin color, general size and shape? If I had been more careful in my sentence construction and avoided the use of the pronoun "he," would you have pictured a person of unknown or non-categorical gender? What does that person look like?

Part of the love philosopher's annotation—typed into a comment bubble in the margin of the syllabus I'd sent—included a description of his ongoing dispute with the author of the article on Love in the *Stanford Encyclopedia of Philosophy.*

He begged me to keep the details confidential, but I am permitted to say that the argument comes down to a foundational difference in the two philosophers' approaches to taxonomy: the author of the article envisions a finite set of categorical distinctions, and so devises those distinctions to cover a prescribed territory beyond which all is dark, while my love philosopher sees no trouble with an open-ended schema—in fact, sees the open-endedness of the schema as itself foundational. It's an argument only philosophers would have with each other.

From the point of view of real-life researchers of love, there's only one side of this schism: the side of the unknown, of risk, of that loss and uncertainty that tie themselves, in both expert and amateur knots, to invention.

I compose a message to the list outlining the debate, not expecting an immediate response. While I'm writing, a couple seated at the table next to me in the café (on the fourth corner, opposite the bodega, the playground, and the apartment) argues in a language I don't know. The couple display an asymmetry: one face stained with contempt and retreat, the other lined with the traces of too much disappointed hope. A stray dog takes pity on the hopeful one, allowing itself to be illicitly, gratefully fed.

I hit Send and shut down, wondering what exactly an open-ended schema would mean.

and I continue to write to S, who soon begins to reply. The two persistent jobs continue to persist in their dissimilar places and ways. My mentor is still absent; the clients' numbers remain undialed in my phone.

The husband and the wife—in my mind—have delayed their talk indefinitely. Or until summer, and summer has arrived.

This procedure of time is not categorically clear: one track moves and another stays still or reverses; the resulting blur makes experience hard to read.

Or: the image of the present has been superimposed on its past and future twins.

(The twins, now, are acting up—the phase of tantrums, the phase of "no.")

Send them outside to work it out. Realign the tracks: mine, theirs, S's, the two groups' (Anti-Love and Love, one intact but soon transforming, one defunct or nearly, but with a digital tail), the syllabi's (official, absorbed, implied), the love philosopher's and the anarchist's and those of the capitalist, my missing mentor, Pablo, and the rest—also the passage of geological time. The days have lengthened. The solstice has come and gone. The mushrooms are fruiting in their bins. The couple from the café stormed off in opposite directions, first the contemptuous one, and then the hopeful one.

This happened months ago, but I'm only remembering it now.

TWO

THE NEWS REPORTS

The Guérillères is a book I possess but do not own.

It was handed to me by a friend in a bookshop: Kansas City, Missouri; or Kansas City, Kansas; or Lawrence.

You'll read it, said the friend, and then return it to me. You have one year, after which the deal is off.

Without specifying the other half of the deal.

I begin it on a subway, and again on a plane, and again on a ferry. It begins the same each time, and each time I remember to add it to the syllabus for Anti-Love. Then I forget, set it aside, pick it up again (on a train). It begins the same.

On the cover: a topless warrior, Medusa-like, swampy grays and greens. Not topless: the warrior's breasts protrude like weapons. As if sharpened on stone.

The clock is ticking. Swipe it from the screen.

Say the Guérillères:

GOLDEN SPACES LACUNAE
THE GREEN DESERTS ARE SEEN
THEY DREAM AND SPEAK OF THEM

RESEARCH

I receive a message from S that contains only a link to a website for the local used bookstore (this is in the city, home of Love, the bodega, playground, and café), and a telegraphic instruction: "Give the desk clerk your name."

It's too early to walk the three blocks to the store, a place where I am known not so much for being a buyer or a browser of books (though I have been both) but for being an old acquaintance of the person most often there tending the tidy shelves and the unruly piles—an acquaintance from a time past, when drugs and love intersected in a clear and particular way in my life, the temporary sway of one leading regularly to the temporary sway of the other via the temporary sway of highly curated, multiply participatory sex.

The bookstore clerk—who was not yet a bookstore clerk but a barkeep—was the director of, and sometimes a participant-observer in, these sessions, connecting the desires of others, instructing, watching, assisting when assistance was needed. The sessions had ended when she disappeared without warning—someone thought Florida, which is where I pictured her for years, when I didn't picture her dead in a gutter somewhere, in the oversize wool sweater her aunt had sent from Peru, also wearing her signature cherry lipstick, her signature lips.

Twelve years later, she showed up at the bookstore, or rather I showed up at the bookstore to find her unaccountably there, and she slipped out from behind the counter to give me a kiss.

I make coffee and shower.

To get dressed without being visible from the playground, the bodega, or the café, I have to position myself behind the door that connects the kitchen to the room where I sleep. I finish the coffee, now cold, and walk the three blocks, arriving just as the grate is being lifted. My clerk isn't there—it's the other clerk, the one with the forgettable name and the memorable hands. Leaning across the piles of books on the counter, the other clerk passes me a small package wrapped in newspaper and twine. "Someone likes you," they declare, deadpan, sitting back down.

At the corner café, I tear open the package. S has written no note to accompany the vintage paperback, which is yellowed and falling apart, tiny shards of brittle paper expelling themselves from its guts and onto my lap. I turn to the first page and read its opening sentence: "Lulu slept naked because she liked to feel the sheets caressing her body and also because laundry was expensive." I read its last sentence: "In the morning, he was always very tender toward himself, his head full of dreams, and broad daylight, cold water, the coarse bristles of the brush made him suffer brutal injustices."

I can't tell how interested I am in knowing what occurs between the two sentences. I close the book. On the cover, a detail from a painting of a woman draped in a blue sheet, her nails and lips red, eyes closed in solipsistic pleasure, or total disinterest, or sleep.

"Unlike anything you've ever read before!" the cover announces. And: *INTIMACY*, in letters redder than the woman's mouth.

⁂

Lulu slept naked because she liked to feel the sheets caressing her body and also because laundry was expensive. What could S be trying to tell me? Was this book on the syllabus, just in a position too far down the list for me to have determined it a priority? I check the document: no *Intimacy*. But that isn't what I really want to know from S.

You wanted a story and I'm sorry, it's difficult, things are not proceeding along linear lines. What other lines exist? Those used to describe impossible objects, tesseracts; lines that stand in for something other than a line, for something *other*.

Not long ago, at lunch with Giorgos, a Greek poet, in a humid garden café in Athens—background, if you let it in: a nation of austerity, collapse, paralyzing debt (swipe, swipe)—the trio of eros, philia, agape is expanded (it's important that Giorgos is Greek). A term gets split, to pry open an impossible space. The new, fourth term gives rise to a question that Giorgos will (he is a talker) readily answer:

"The fourth term—*erotas*—gets added in order to protect eros from itself. What is the difference? Erotas disorients extremely, but temporarily. We all know what that's like: you can think of nothing else. But when it vanishes, it's as if a fever has broken—the *fact* of it may remain in memory but the feeling, the sensation, becomes instantly inaccessible. We all know that too." A pause as we sip our coffee, which has somehow grown cooler than the thick midsummer air. I ask: "And eros? I understand what it's being rescued from, but for what is it being saved?"

There is no pause, this time. "Eros, real eros, doesn't disorient; it rather *re*orients. Definitively." He grins—"Or so I've heard, at least"—and waves his hand to summon the bill.

⚬

You, too, have questions. Where are we in time and space? For example. Some answers are easy: It's summer. I am in the corner apartment, alone, for a week; my part-time roommates are away;

the café-bar in the village to the north is temporarily closed so the plumbing can be repaired. I have one last push with my job for the capitalist, one more paycheck on the way.

Other answers are less forthcoming. The trick—like the joke where the drunk keeps hunting for his keys in the wrong place, a phenomenon referenced earnestly in the mediation manual as "the Streetlight Effect"—is not to look only where the light falls.

When I said that Pablo is needed now, I am referencing an event that will occur but hasn't yet.

Another term for the Streetlight Effect is "the Drunkard's Search."

⚓

It has happened, the talk between the husband and the wife, a season or two behind schedule. It was efficient and it was kind. (The scene appeared; I couldn't help it, anymore than I could, without dialing their numbers, help those performing it.)

"There are two types of people," said the wife to the husband, or said the husband to the wife.

"There's the type of person who hates to fly in a passenger plane, because to do so means putting your life in the hands of a stranger, and letting chance—booking agents, online travel sites, all the different reasons people pass through the same place—determine the last faces you will behold before you die. And there's the type who loves to fly—the longer and higher and more turbulent, the better—precisely because of these circumstances. Because handing it all over is an ecstasy, a balm."

Of course, we know there are more than these two kinds of people, including those who are indifferent to flying and those who have never flown, so don't know. But this wasn't a thorough exploration. This was a talk that was over before it began: an emblem of all that was irreconcilable between the wife and the husband, and also a story about two people who love each other but who are no longer in love sitting together on a plane.

⚮

Only now may S return to the scene, by writing a letter that will arrive—this is a story about fate, or coincidence—on the same day as a new email from the capitalist.

Two letters, one on paper and one delivered to a screen, at dusk, as the last children exit the playground accompanied by their adults, the streetlights shudder and alight, and the bodega owner steps outside for a cigarette.

I reach for a cigarette. This is a story about free will.

THE NEWS REPORTS

A Dialogue on Love is a book I ordered used from the internet after reading about a different book by the same author in a book by a different author whom I didn't know personally but who struck me as kindred at the time.

In *A Dialogue,* which tells the story of a love theorist and her experience with psychoanalysis, which includes what appear to be intact quotations from the analyst's notebook written in real time, a formal strategy announces itself on the first page and continues to the end.

Small poems—not always but often approximations of haiku—
interrupt the flow of the prose
as if not to let us get too comfortable (in the flow of the prose) in the story
of the (therapeutic, therefore intimate) relationship developing between the analyst and the analysand, each of whom reveals themselves, from the beginning (of the book, which may not be the beginning of the story) to possess the emotional receptors required for the necessary bond to quickly, deeply form. Still, it is not until page thirty-nine that the interruption admits, in so many words:

"If I can't kick this
　　　　door open, there isn't hope—"

TWO LETTERS

The letter—an email, technically—from the capitalist began, unsurprisingly, "Dear Colleagues" and ended "Yours, &c," a flourish that, despite myself, I found charming. (What is charming about the old-fashioned, ever? Especially when found in a smiling, towering capitalist with eyes that sparkle like fairy dust? This, too, is among the questions being asked, though differently aspected, by both Love and Anti-Love.)

In the middle of the letter a sentence stood out, by which I mean a sentence appeared to have been tucked away for those who might bother to find it. It was a long sentence, uncharacteristic of the capitalist as I knew him, but it was positioned between short ones containing just the pieces of information that would call out to any readers who were skimming the email for such—the "Co-Lab" session will take place at which media conglomerate's headquarters, at what hour, and whether this time we would be required to provide one or two pieces of photo ID to be let through the blinking lights of the secured turnstiles—and he'd even bothered to tag onto the end of the sentence itself a morsel of informative content that was also meant to be skimmed:

"I have been pondering the use-value of this program to the extent of wondering if our efforts, as cofacilitators, to provide divergent points of view on the subject may be backfiring, a case of too many competing flavors creating a tasteless or an untasteable stew, and I wonder if we should have a conversation about this, which come to think of it reminds me that we had requests for more vegan options at the Co-Lab lunch, so I've arranged for a greater number of the pizzas to be cheese free."

I don't want to credit the capitalist with intending to introduce a question that—only when unmoored from its context and applied to others—feels so close to one I have returned to frequently without ever managing to articulate it: What is the difference between the tasteless and the untasteable?

It will seem strange to claim this question, of all others, as a summary of our conversations in Anti-Love. But if you think about it, if you draw it as a diagram, doesn't the difference have everything to do with learned desire?

And then, from S:

"Dear E, I wanted to send you something through time and space, and through a network of anarchically organized bodies with history. Futurity? Maybe also. But it will be short, this. Telegraphic, even.

"I am reading, and everything I read seems to belong to our syllabus. I'm working too much. The restaurant has been crazed. The people moving to this neighborhood never thought they'd leave center city, and they walk around looking for a familiar perch from which to look out at what's unfamiliar to them—at the people who lived here before they arrived and before the people who made them feel they could move here had arrived. I'm in the middle, not truly from here but not a newcomer either. I guess I'm one of those people who *made them feel they could* (etc.). An accidental translator for an interim period. We just spring up, like clover, which permaculture calls a *pioneer*. I'll be crowded out soon by more substantial plants. I deserve it!

"So, these fragile monolingual lilies were resting at the outdoor tables, scanning the street for something recognizable or comforting, and there was a lull, no bell from the kitchen expected for a bit, so I went back to my book, which I have been opening at random, no bookmark, couldn't tell you why. The book is called *G.*—it came up in a search for 'Don Juan' (I was trying to expand the syllabus). But I can't tell what it's about, not really, the way I'm reading around in it. It's pleasing.

"One day I'll send you something I've written myself (maybe). But for now, here is a paragraph from *G.* that I found myself wanting to copy out and send to you in my hand.

"Yrs, S"

A DIAGRAM

A COPIED PARAGRAPH

"The crowd see the city around them with different eyes. They have stopped the factories producing, forced the shops to shut, halted the traffic, occupied the streets. It is they who have built the city and they who maintain it. They are discovering their own creativity. In their regular lives they only modify presented circumstances; here, filling the streets and sweeping all before them they oppose their very existence to circumstances. They are rejecting all that they habitually, and despite themselves, accept. Once again they demand together what none can ask alone: Why should I be compelled to sell my life bit by bit so as not to die?"

It has been some time since my mentor disappeared. Enough time to stop expecting my attempts at contact to be returned, enough time to stop initiating new attempts, but not enough time to feel certain that the disappearance is permanent.

My life, which had once been wide, funded by rootlessness, luck, and credit, founded on worn narratives of progress and its critique (surely the very notion of apprenticing at all would imply a belief in the existence of a future), has become, suddenly, narrower. Less mobile. It occurs to me that if my apprenticeship has in fact ended, then once my obligations with the capitalist are complete, I will be handing in my notice at the shared corner apartment. I will be needing, while also perhaps wanting, to stay put in the place in which my life is, on the whole, more manageable. To stay put out of chance and necessity, but also to learn what the fact of *staying put* might mean.

It occurs to me that before this happens, I would like to create an opportunity to meet S in person; at the same time, I feel certain that the moment has not yet come.

For now, my week at the apartment is up and I have a shift tomorrow back at the café-bar.

⚜

It occurs to me that S knows just as little about my body, about my tangible self, as I know about theirs. Soon S will again be 150 miles away.

WHO WE ARE

Last night, in a contemplative mood, or mode, I harvested one of the mushrooms from the bin and bit off the cap.

I was hoping to find a shortcut to discovering what it is I want to tell you. About my questions and my lists, about the unsecured corporate wireframe and the terribly tender flesh.

I lay down and had a very long sentence foot under then over leg to the window where one no two trees hid a brightbright thing, starthing faraway green though up close were also a thousand-hundred or hunnerred smaller that looked the same size and the dog—did you know there was a dog, not a real—was a waggything and then, and then it became allclear, because this was mild, you see, only a smallsmall bite, and now it's morning and I'm clever and it's time to tell you who I am.

Or who I'm not: myself. Is that enough?

Ten days ago, at a summer fair—fried dough, bouncy castle, corn dogs and crystals and soap—I ran into one of the members of Anti-Love. We are on hiatus for the summer—actually, we have finished the collection of essays on our syllabus, and we've been so careful about power sharing that everyone is reluctant to weigh in on what to read next. There was a tentative offering about prisons. One about communes. One about gray water and composting toilets, with several hands-on workdays figured in. (Were we finished with theory? We pinned black discs to our shirts, placeholders for the next protest. Some of us had read *Fragments of an Anarchist*

Anthropology and been moved by its argument for localized practice, for methods named after processes themselves rather than after the men who'd thought them up.)

Or, what would it mean not to be finished with theory? We had found our members—including the one I saw at the fair and hugged through sweat and smiles—by stapling a flyer to a telephone pole.

The "we" is royal.

The flyer said: ARE YOU TIRED OF INVENTION, TIRED OF HISTORY, DO YOU FEEL THAT YOU'RE ALL OUT OF FIGHT? COME SIT AND READ ANGRY THINGS WITH OTHER ANGRY PEOPLE. MAYBE IT WILL FEEL LIKE LOVE. NO FASCISTS. BEER. COFFEE. FREE.

Who I am (cont'd): a person who can't tell time, can't tell it what to do, can't figure anything; one who can't stop looking out the window—currently, a window on a train, the same train on which I began, for the third time, *The Guérillères,* the same window, too, but a different date on the calendar, a different number on my ten-ride pass; a person who has swallowed so much rage over the years that anger has become conflated with food, seasoned by paralysis and grief (a person who suspects any extended metaphor out of hand); a person who is suspicious, even, of the word *person* and all it suggests (especially preceded by a definite or indefinite article) about the separation between entities or their separability, and one who tests this separation regularly by all the usual means: projection, depersonalization, a certain porousness that isn't always safe to maintain, a certain obsession, an addiction to this simple act of looking (as out the window from a train); a person who is driven, in real time, to the subject at hand—to the composite Janus face of Love and Anti-Love (placeholders, we know, for forms that express themselves multiply, in corporate wireframes and in terribly tender flesh)—driven by a lifetime, a muddle, a lifetime of muddles on the way to a theory or an anti-theory (jury's still out); an anarchic person, seeking solace and company and lust, possibly a restorative beating, figurative or not; and a person who is more interested, finally, in who you are.

Consider this a message in a bottle. Consider it a fossil, a remain. A text.

%

Who you are: we don't know. The pronouns are problematic. The problems are pronominal: you are you because not-me, not-I, not-we. I love you and I don't know why. Can't say why. You are the idea of the question, the vested idea. The poison and the gift.

are too innumerable to record. We do not exist in a vacuum, despite the presumption and desire, on the part of those in charge, that we remain incapable of recognizing what we are a part of, the roles in which we've been cast.

The anger and despair that gave rise—let's be honest—to both Love and Anti-Love did not themselves arise in a vacuum, don't feed on air alone. I could list the ambient and direct forces acting on each of us in this story, these stories, I could track their crescendos as they leave record after record in the dust, or I could let you list them yourself, in the margins of this or of one of the books in your own stack.

If I prefer, if I choose, the latter, it's not only out of lassitude or nervousness about the inadequacy of my efforts (my current limits); it's also out of a stubborn belief in the power of marginalia. It must be the case that, under certain conditions, the margins can rewrite the text.

Because the universe itself was rearranging, individuals began rearranging their own universes as well, not only the husband and the wife coming apart but other husbands and wives, and husbands and husbands and wives and wives, and pairs of people who had eschewed the institution of marriage but who had entered other institutions of their own design, of care and resource sharing and of rules and infractions—all of these were sent into a new state of entropy, of comings-apart and comings-together, as if riding the crest of the universe-level changes that were, with ever-increasing velocity, on the approach—an approach everyone sensed but no one could satisfyingly articulate.

The question arose also, not only with Pablo and his reluctant former partner in non-primacy, not only in the writings of the anarchist or of the other anarchists, of whether the dyad or the private family could possibly be the way to weather the approaching storm.

These weren't new questions: in Anti-Love we had read not one but many dozens of arguments against the tyranny of the pair, of pairing, of the couple before the invention of marriage and, certainly, after it, many dating back hundreds if not thousands of years. Now, in some circles, the popularization of this choice to break with habit and finally dismantle the *traditional family*—this politics' slow and incomplete migration from the active margins to the passive core—was cast in sensationalist family-values messaging as *the nuclear option*. A weak joke: it was more like the *anti*-"nuclear" option (a linguistic knot familiar to both Love and Anti-Love).

To the capitalist, I replied privately: "I vote against vegan pizza and for vegan salad." To S, I related the news about the various disintegrations, the rampant decouplings and recouplings and the thinking that surrounded them, ending my letter with a short postscript: "Did you know that in chemistry, a dyad is a divalent chemical, a *radical*?"

(While we were reading, in Anti-Love, about the near-inevitable and total failures of the romantically bonded pair, somewhere in the memories of the members of Love who predated my invitation to the group lived the remnants of a discussion—there must have been a discussion—about the second text on their syllabus, one of three inclusions from ancient Greece, the one containing the argument between Socrates and Aristophanes in which the latter proposes a primal division of one into two, followed by the lifelong search for a reunion between separated halves. Two halves make a whole. As if math. As if chemistry. In my reconstruction of the scene, Love's members turn to this question: whether, if Aristophanes was right, the dyad, radical in the literal sense, could become radical, too, in the political sense that—months later, in a different locale with a different climate and altitude and economy—formed the center of so many discussions in Anti-Love.)

What I did, instead of following this convoluted thought further, was pack my notebooks and sunscreen and my jacketless hardbound copy of *The Psychedelic Reader* into my bag and head for the corner café.

It was crowded. It is crowded: I find a table next to a woman who is sitting quietly, reading a book I don't recognize—I can't even discern the type of book, it's incognito, which means she, too, is incognito—but who, as soon as I settle in beside her, begins to cough painfully, desperately, at length, preventing me from remembering that I had a plan for my time here (a plan for paragraphs to compose, pages to read).

I put my fingers to my mouth—unconsciously—and recognize, from the inside, a pose. What is the pose of thinking? An embarrassment, for one. But also a sign of suspense, or suspension, between the first recognition of a knot and the first intuition about how it might be made to come apart.

THE NEWS REPORTS

I am not going to report on the book I picked up from the stack,
opened, and began to read, then put down, with its bright-patterned
cover, background lilac or rose, brighter flowers abstracted and
bleeding to the edge, title scrawled in a deep orange red above, in
smaller lettering, the name of my faraway friend. I'm not going

to copy his beautiful opening line about sexual
pleasure and
reading. I'm going to report, telegraphically, on the actual
news, dominated today by the march
of the white supremacists
the countermarch of the anti–white supremacists
the think piece about white supremacy
the behavior of the white supremacists
the behavior of the pigs, so like
the behavior of the white supremacists
the behavior of the larger group of anti–white supremacists
who were nonetheless
by the calculus of power
outnumbered.

I've been avoiding the news in these news reports, reaching instead
for the new, an attempt to pry

it out, from remains, from
bibliomancy.

You aren't surprised; you know by now how I am.

I'm going to pick up the book again, the one with the pink
cover, shiny, tear-proof, and read the second line
and then the third.

CASTING

I dream about S. A dream that vanished on waking, then rebuilt itself, image by image and sensation by sensation, a series of affective aftershocks that continued for several hours of the day. At first I thought I might be dreaming as either the husband or the wife: the dream could have belonged to either, with a near inevitability; it may have helped one or both to move forward, or sideways— something. But it was, truly, about S, at least as much as a dream can be said to be *about* a person impossible to picture, impossible to represent.

S was simply present, infused in the narrative without being cast in it exactly.

Casting, after all, is what S seems to exist to avoid.

The scene was like an animated card from the tarot, a symbolic illustration come to something-like-life. Its setting was a rectangular stone-lined pool in the courtyard of a crumbling house, once grand and large enough for several dyads, triads, and multiples—a potential site for the anti-nuclear option, though all markers (markers that were sensed rather than observed or read) pointed toward a lonely past of opulent but unused, light-filled rooms. Back in the courtyard, a shallow pool: a *reflecting pool* that, covered in duckweed or some other pond scum, refused to reflect.

I was there—(Were you? There was a diffuse and haunted sense of being observed from somewhere in the house, above the courtyard.)—but I was there in the pool, looking down at the scum, trying to locate, to decipher, something that could pass for my reflection. The scene froze there.

What made it unfreeze is the part I don't understand.

Something—some possession, some spell, the words are hard to use—occurred, and I began to lift my right foot. The effort this took was enormous.

As I struggled, another element entered my visual field, in the upper register, above my right eyebrow: a graphic scale of exertion, like those posters hung on doctors' walls—a horizontal, timeline-style bar, glowing and hovering like a surtitle to the scene. The scale was an invitation to interpret my experience: it depicted, in increasing orders of magnitude, the amount of effort it should take to draw a foot from water; the amount it should take to draw a foot from mud; the amount from tar; from quicksand; the amount of effort that can be mustered only with a full-blown flight response, an adrenaline shot; the amount of effort on the face of women in videos of childbirth or of men in videos of the effects of taking PCP. At the top of the scale (its rightmost edge): the kind of effort that is so great it becomes invisible, as if to show it on your face would be to rob the muscles that need the body's energy the most. Intuiting this, I remained impassive. I made the effort, raised my foot—I shocked myself. My left foot followed, less laboriously, and I dragged my lower half with my upper, leaning forward in a deep, hinged lunge, through three giant paces to the pool's edge, which faced the vaulted double doors of the decaying house. There was a set of two shallow stone steps leading out of the pool; they nearly killed me.

Or, they killed me. In pain, I screamed myself awake.

S was there, but how, where, in what form? S as gravity or surface tension or the combination of both, challenging me like a coach would, to "find my inner strength"?

Or S as pond scum, sadistic, daring me to accuse them of something. (But of what? Of holding, of withholding?)

Or—the simplest interpretation, and the hardest to ignore: S as deus ex machina, as chemistry: adrenaline, PCP.

And what, neglected syllabus, does this have to do with Love?

AN INSTABILITY

The neglected syllabus, the one for Love (I never neglected Anti-Love; I was stalwart and read every word), which was hosted on the cloud and was unstable, with adjustments made weekly, contained these names in this order:

Stanford Encyclopedia of Philosophy
Plato
Aristotle
Sir Thomas Aquinas
La Rochefoucauld
Danto
Milton
Goldman
Hegel
Schopenhauer
Lawrence
Stendhal
Rousseau
Nietzsche
Freud
Spinoza
Ovid
Shakespeare
Lacan
Klein
Deleuze

Bersani
Foucault
Austin
Barthes
Sedgwick
Kraus
hooks
Leconte
Berlant
Badiou

It isn't that I didn't read any of it. It's that I wanted, I want, a different syllabus. Not just different, but different in *kind*. And I get stranded in the gap between editing and starting a new file.

So here's a story I know how to tell: a fantasy—not a dream, a fantasy that filled the precise duration of this morning's train ride between the (former) locale of Love and the (also now former, though for different reasons, and only temporarily) locale of Anti-Love. A fantasy I finally had about the capitalist.

A FANTASY

He is a tall man: a cis man, a straight man, a freewheeling, grinning, doe-eyed, gentle-dad, go-to-the-key-party-but-leave-your-keys-in-your-pocket man. Olive skinned, from some combination of countries that all border warm, salted seas. He claimed once, in passing, never to have pulled an all-nighter to meet a deadline.

An organized man. An organization man. A kind of man who thinks he wants you to call his bluff. I found myself wondering: What would that mean?

I found myself letting the wondering extend into something more vivid than wondering: a model, to scale, of an encounter intended to perform the extraction of pleasure I'd felt the urge to accomplish those months ago.

He lies before me, on a bed of sand: the sandbox in the playground across from the bodega and the café, a sandbox shunned by germophobic parents in a playground from which the childless (we call them—ourselves—the child-free, in Anti-Love) are forbidden entry; but it is after hours. His eyes are closed, his head—close-cropped black hair, two-day stubble—is turned gently to the left, to face in toward the seesaw and climbing bars, away from the streetlights. His lips form an inscrutable smile, like what I imagine would be found on a wealthy, professionally primped corpse. His arms and legs are splayed, his expensive jeans fully tented at the crotch. He's wearing a putty-green T-shirt bearing a vaguely retro logo in yellow, some tech start-up or indie-rock band or just a corporate clothing-chain simulacrum of either. I want it off, but without disturbing his well-positioned limbs.

⚬

I have said that this fantasy is a fantasy about the extraction of pleasure from a capitalist, as a form (I understood at the time) of redress, of compensation. And I haven't even yet begun to describe the unfolding event to you—my toolbox and its deployment, and the capitalist's response—but before going on, I need to say something more about fantasy than what this scenario would suggest.

In Anti-Love, I once shared an additional reading—nobody else bit, but that's not unusual—which included this claim: "It is well known that stout persons throughout the ages have found that they had some sense of freedom, even an enhanced sense of freedom, when in states of physical restraint."

What needs asking is how this proposition, if it is correct, might alter my intent: if freedom is pleasure, or if it is related to pleasure, then I can know what I'm doing to the capitalist, in the sandbox, after hours, only to the extent to which I understand his relation to the formulation above.

Don't we know already that pleasure is not transferable like cash? Between participants in a scene like this one, who or what owns any surplus pleasure that might result? How much of a difference— qualitative, or quantitative—does it make if it turns out that, contra expectations, a fantasy is shared?

I am visited by Giorgos the Greek, leaning forward across his cup of cold coffee, urging me on: "Yes, exactly, if the fantasy is shared, and whether fleetingly or not—that is the axis on which we determine the difference between eros and erotas!"

I am visited by the report from my friend about her theorist— "He said *gather*"—

❧

I take his hand and turn it over, palm up. Is freedom transferable? Is that the same as asking if it's zero-sum?

❧

I want the shirt off, but without disturbing his well-positioned limbs, so I open my toolbox—a metal lunch pail, matte black, bearing the logo for *M*A*S*H,* a family heirloom (don't ask)—and choose the smaller of my two pairs of scissors, start to snip.

An instant before reaching the neckline, I have an intuition, a vision, that there will be nipple piercings—it's not that I want them, I just know they'll be there. And when I separate the two halves of the capitalist's T-shirt, two deep-brown nipples pierced with standard hoop-and-ball rings are revealed, set in a field of sparse, salt-and-pepper parentheses of hair.

Is the fantasy shared? There is always an obvious place to go— you're going there now, the rings are ready to be threaded with something, some cord or twine or dental floss, pulled from the domed lunch box. A scene in which the slow and steady applica- tion of pressure—or, in this case, a pulling, which amounts to the opposite of pressure, in diametric relation as dehydration is to drowning—creates the conditions for a limit state.

"Trust me," I say to the capitalist, though not yet speaking aloud. "You like to trust; you sleep easily—don't you?—like a baby."

Instead of reaching for rope or twine, for a strand or two of the landscaping grass that edges the sandbox in the newly renovated playground, I grab the rings with my fingers and, very slowly, begin to pull.

"You know Kahneman, right?" I ask the capitalist, whose body has perceptibly stiffened in response to my action. "You brought him up when we were designing the session on decision architecture." He nods, then turns his head to face me, makes a point of engaging my eyes, but no more words come.

"Describe to me," I say, pulling a little harder on each ring, "the peak-end rule." A tiny smile forms on his face as he turns it away again, again making me think of a made-up corpse; the smile, as I pull up one more fraction of an inch, flickers to a grimace.

"The peak-end rule describes a multiply tested and experimentally verified phenomenon," he begins as I pull incrementally on his nipples, their tents becoming smaller versions in duplicate of the tent at his crotch, which is not remaining stagnant but is itself wavering, trembling, undecided about which direction it's headed, "in which the values of experienced pain and of remembered pain are pitted against each other, causing a" (he emits a small gasp in response to another pull) "*conundrum* where decisions pitting quantity and quality of pain are concerned."

In response to another tug, his hands are on my forearms, not pulling them away, just freezing them. A tear rolls from the corner of his left eye into his left nostril (his head is still in profile, cheek on the sand). I let him slowly, incrementally, lower my arms and watch as all three tents deflate. (Why am I spending this time on the capitalist? Accessibility, availability, lack of imagination, perhaps. Also, it's been some time since I've heard from S; I'm lonely.)

When I remove my hands from the rings, he takes a long breath in and out, and tent number one begins to rise again.

ఞ

The train conductor walks by, chanting the name of my station and pulling the little card on which its initials are inscribed from the rail above my head. Good-bye, sparkling river view. Good-bye, capitalist. Good-bye, nipples and parenthetical hair. Good-bye—oh, good-bye tent, before you have had the chance to fully raise yourself. "Five minutes, five minutes," says the conductor. "Exit to the rear."

The voices of two women who must have boarded, or found their way to the café car, while I was deep in my fantasy about the capitalist are suddenly unbearably present behind my left shoulder. ". . . And at the party, he doesn't look at me, he's flirting with that woman's cousin—she's so young!—and everyone keeps telling me how lucky he is, how beautiful I am, how exotic, you know, they don't know anyone from South America, but he's all over this blond . . ." "I would be livid! Livid!" "And so you know what I did? I dragged his ass out dancing the next night and you should see the dress I wore, oh wait, I have a picture . . ."

I gathered my things, not easy because of their heterogenous shapes and materials—"Are you kidding? He did *not!*"—and exited, bag on shoulder, unpacked belongings in hand.

ఞ

The peak-end rule is a psychological heuristic in which people judge an experience largely based on how they felt at its peak (i.e., its most intense point) and at its end, rather than based on the total sum or average of every moment of the experience.

According to the peak-end rule, our memory of past experience (pleasant or unpleasant) does not correspond to an average level of positive or negative feelings but to the most extreme point and the end of the episode.

Discover how the cognitive bias of the peak-end rule influences you to make terrible life choices, and how you can use it to your advantage.

Use this simple psychology rule to improve your customers' experience.

Happiness: it's all about the ending.

WOUNDS

When I told you to look out for the peak-end scene I imagined with the capitalist, I was thinking about reading, and love of reading, and of the sword that leaves a scar when reading draws us in and then, unceremoniously, kicks us out. With a pronoun, a slur, or some other reminder of the text's ambient, violent ground.

What I may have been thinking was that in the most extreme cases of this phenomenon, our recollection of a beloved text reduces into two ends of a continuum—reduces, that is, to the highest point of pleasure and identity with it, and to the lowest point, the gut-kick of exclusion. (The end.)

This may explain the blur of partial recall—love plus rage plus shame.

This may be the point of kicking open the door.

But S has begun to challenge me on exactly this point. I wasn't able to recognize it at first; my defenses were triggered, and for a time, weeks maybe, they worked. But defenses wear down and eventually crack, revealing vulnerabilities (this is, from a different angle, a description of the phenomenon described by the sword/ scar/blur).

It began—the challenge—after I sent my notes following receipt of the paragraph S had copied from *G.*, in which I described the experience triggered by my rereading of Pascal. What S challenged was the value of doing so in the first place. What S challenged was the value even of giving thought to, spending the energy of analysis on, this experience—which, from my description of it, registered mostly as discomfort—at all.

Is it possible that S feels about me the way I feel about the capitalist? If true, is it possible S may have a point?

I had these thoughts during a shift at the café-bar. It was even slower than usual, and I'd taken out my laptop, which sat closed on the counter.

I felt something like love for S, and S felt something for me—this I knew, I sensed, without doubt. I was suddenly sleepy, fatigued by this wondering, blasted by a sharp new ray of sun through the glass door. A sentence arrived as I let my eyes drop shut: Is it possible to love someone who doesn't share your wounds, someone whose wounds are so different from your own?

It so happened that the day of the train fantasy and the arrival at the peak-end rule was also a day in which, just before dinner and after my journey was complete, a video call was scheduled between me and the capitalist and our other colleagues, those of us who participated in the online scheduling poll.

That day is today. That call is now. I'll be right back.

THE NEWS REPORTS

Living a Feminist Life is a book I listened to in a car, almost exclusively during trips back and forth between the village in which Anti-Love met and the station stop at which I habitually boarded a train to the city in which Love met, or had once met, before my time.

It's a good book to listen to. Like *A Dialogue on Love,* it uses poetry to interrupt the presumed (if false) transparency of nonfiction prose. By poetry I mean poetic techniques: meter, rhyme, homonym, repetition, iteration, recursion, and something harder to describe, some relation of sound to sense that keeps the reader perpetually
        thrown.

But *Living a Feminist Life* is not a poem; it is an indoctrination.

I vow to give it to my next pregnant friend, cued up on padded headphones (or ones made especially for pregnant
bellies—someone
must be peddling those by now).

Fuck Mozart: play *this* to that disaster in the making, to that grotesque and unbearable signifier of hope.

FLUCTUATIONS

The continual back-and-forth, the never-really-touching-ground, can make it seem like life is happening elsewhere. And then sometimes you're reminded that, in fact, it is.

My mentor called. I was crouched down behind the counter at the café-bar, rummaging in the disorderly shelves for a packet of artificial sweetener while my impatient customer, a stranger, sighed audibly above my head.

It was a poor connection, digitized and lossy. Holding the phone to my ear with my shoulder, finally putting my hands on a little pink packet and standing up to give it to the stranger, who seemed poised for defeat, I tried to decipher what I could hear of my mentor's words.

"Not sure when," my mentor said.

"Total mess," my mentor said.

"Rely on the Manual," my mentor said, and then, "but trust yourself."

HEAT

The heat index is at 103 degrees—though summer is nearly over—in the city in which Love used to meet, and the apartment is a diagram of airflow under constant revision: fans set to "in" or "exhaust" in hopeful rotation from window to window, a sole insufficient air conditioner inconveniently placed over the sink in the kitchen, a small crank-operated skylight that may or may not be effective at letting hot air escape through the roof. I am looking for a novel that I suspect the bookstore might have in stock, so I put on as little as I can get away with in public and enter the street.

The feeling is like pushing a mattress with my torso. Each one of us on the street, pushing our own mattress: when we pass too closely to ignore one another completely, we peek our heads around our personal burdens and sneak an occasional shared grimace or smile, then push on.

At the store, the clerk with the memorable hands greets me; we make rote mention of climate disaster and of the morning's news.

Then they wink and say: "She's downstairs, working on inventory. I'm sure she'd love a visit."

Downstairs is a cramped black-box theater where fiction and poetry readings take place when the weather turns cold, making the more inviting backyard unusable. But until November or so, the tiny black-painted stage serves as a sorting platform for incoming used books. Sometimes, after a bibliophile has died—as two local ones just have, one from cancer, one from apparent suicide—the stacks reach the height of a person.

My clerk is not in the theater, though, but in the even more minuscule adjacent "office," with the lights off and an old freestanding AC roaring, her outline illuminated by the glow of an on-screen spreadsheet.

She stands up and turns around, having sensed me in the doorway, and in turning around she turns time back nearly twenty years; we're in the walk-in cooler at the restaurant, it's the middle of an endless, cocaine-fueled Saturday-night shift, a shift we know will end with several of us naked on the carpeted floor of the head waiter's apartment; it's not the beginning but not quite the middle of the slow buildup that, though predictable because habitual, is still the best method we've invented for fighting the more deadly predictability of its obedient alternative: punch in, punch out, count tips, go home. We, the clerk and I, are suddenly there, which means we're suddenly kissing, half-laughing, seriously joking or joking seriously about the insistence of injecting bodily pleasure into a place of work. By the time she slides her hand down the front of my skirt, the joke has won and we're only laughing, no longer kissing even; she extracts her hand and we hug each other and rock back and forth, now teary, the embrace we were too stunned to perform the day I walked into the bookstore and found her unaccountably there and that on our subsequent meetings would have seemed arbitrary, out of sequence. She says, "I'm off at five, you free for a drink?" and I say I am, and I go back upstairs and look for the book I want, and find it.

I fell in love during the time of my clerk's well-curated sessions, but not with the clerk herself. This was a thing that only ever went so far, a groove that (we now know) has not been entirely filled in by time. So it isn't exactly that we have unfinished business. But I'd thought she was dead. And the more I think about her prior art form in relation to Love and Anti-Love, the more questions I have.

I keep failing to address the insufficiency, the wrongness, of the name "Anti-Love." And of "Love," for that matter. Maybe I missed my chance at the beginning. Maybe I'll get to it later. Maybe I assume it's obvious to you. I won't fail, though, to address my questions to the clerk, now that I have the chance.

The bar is air-conditioned, so I arrive early to cool off, take out my notebook and a pen.

QUESTIONS FOR A CLERK

When you were positioning us on the rug and guiding our engage-
ments with each other, were you thinking about our pleasure, or
your pleasure, or the pleasure of one of us over the other of us, or is
it possible you weren't thinking about pleasure at all? Did you wear
that bright lipstick so you could mark each one of us; was it a thrill
to see its traces, like an artist autographing her work? Did it bother
you when we all, or when some of us, had done too much blow and
lost interest or just wanted to talk? Did you care when someone had
done too much dope and couldn't get it up, or couldn't come? Did it
embarrass you when you misread someone's availability for a particular kink?

The questions were such obvious ones I grew bored by them; I
grow bored. It's too cold in here. But it's too hot out there. She's
late, by a half hour, more. I get that feeling that happens when a
blizzard makes you miss the party you didn't know you wanted
to miss.

As I'm contemplating leaving, a chorus of grating, upper-register
bleets, along with the sound of phones vibrating on hard surfaces,
overtakes the bar. I think, for the first time in decades, about what
we learned in grade school to call Mexican jumping beans (Were
they Mexican? Were they beans?) and look around at the handful
of afternoon drinkers (startled) and their collaborators behind the
bar (nonplussed), and then I look at my blinking phone, an emergency flash-flood alert, just as the sky starts to pummel the bar's
metal roof with rain.

THE NEWS REPORTS

The book I removed from my bag while stranded at the bar beneath pummeling rain—Yuri Herrera's *Signs Preceding the End of the World,* translated from Spanish by Lisa Dillman—was the book I had wanted to find at the bookstore before visiting my clerk in its basement, and it was the book I did find when I returned upstairs after our nostalgic session of groping-turned-laughter had run its course. I remove it from my bag and set it next to my notebook and pen.

Stood up, now, by my clerk and stranded by rain, in one-hundred-degree heat, in a bar in which, it becomes clear (first by semi-conscious deduction, later confirmed by mutual interrogation) most of the dozen people present are un- or underemployed—

stood up, not surprised or even disappointed at being stood up, but still affected—

still, despite myself, a little turned on, by the clerk's hand having been down my skirt, by the contextualizing laughter itself, turned

on, also, by the book I've just bought, the cover of which is seductive matte black, a night
landscape with dunes, cactus—

a small and violent, generous book (from the text on the back: I'm pointing again, it's a habit, I know), the kind I make an effort to find when someone trusted tips me off—

I am struck by the scene, its unlikeliness: the unexpected rain and the intensity of it (you really can't go outside in this; the streets are empty), the unexpected encounter with my believed-to-be-dead clerk, even the near-instant change of tenor among my cohabitants in the bar, who went from silent to annoyed to convivial (with one exception: the bartender, scowling and swiping at her screen) five minutes into the deluge. Struck

by the scene, and just staring at the book and its title. I don't know what it's about, not really. I open it to page one of section one, "The Earth":

"I'm dead, Makina said to herself when everything lurched."

THE ACTUAL NEWS

What the actual news reports said, when the bartender turned on the television twenty minutes into the downpour, was that this was a tropical storm—Ezekiel—that had surprised the meteorologists by straying farther west than expected and now risked being upgraded to a hurricane, screwing with the nomenclature, it turns out, since in the U.S., tropical storms and hurricanes are named by different bodies, governmental and non (a fact the flustered meteorologist spent a minute of screen time on while sedans and SUVs floated down roiling street-rivers from left to right across the bar's oversize TV).

I looked around. I look around: to my right, three lone drinkers, each pounding thumbs or fingers against a phone. To my left, a pair, youthful in dress and posture though I can't see the age-betraying parts—faces, hands—so glued together are they in lips and tongues and, it turns out when I look harder, tears. They don't seem to be fighting. One keeps grabbing the other's chest, twisting T-shirt between fingers, which appears to make the other cry harder and also kiss harder. One is blond with a pink streak sprouting from the temple, the other wears a deep-black ponytail. I'm still staring at them, wanting to know what they know, when everything lurches.

⚘

It isn't that I made a decision, after the unexpected but seismically "minor" storm-trailing quake, to get back on a train with the river to my left and let the city recede behind me. It's that Leslie, one of the members of Anti-Love, sent out an invitation to a double-feature home screening of *Gaslight* (1940) and *Gaslight* (1944)—films we'd discovered almost none of us knew, though the verb "to gaslight" had come up both casually and as a subject of scrutiny in several of our meetings—with a promise to share her fresh harvest of two Gas & Guns plants and one new-to-her strain called Shimmer. I was due back the next day anyway; I just caught an earlier train.

The train was replete with commuters, a time slot I usually avoid. Usually avoided. People returning to their suburban and exurban homes after a day at the office inspired petty judgement of a kind I would rather not be forced to feel: an unholy blend of pity, contempt, and self-incrimination tempered by a doomed tenderness.

In the end Ezekiel had caused little but traffic problems in the city, but as the train moved northward and I was able to transfer my attention from the depressed commuters ("Why should I be compelled to sell my life bit by bit so as not to die?") to my habitual eavesdropping on the conductors and café staff, I became aware that the storm had wreaked significantly more havoc in the north, a realization that morphed from hearsay to fact as the landscape on the non-river side was overtaken more and more by the dying limbs of downed trees, chopped into chunks by the highway or train service and stacked in zoomorphic heaps by the tracks' edge.

How the cloudscape out the window of a moving train's café car, heavy gray and low, is frame by frame animated behind the car's live action, how the attention of the viewer takes it all in simultaneously, foreground and background and asynchronous surround-ground, how you could describe it as aspect to aspect rather than moment to moment, like a Miyazaki film, how you could describe it like a dream.

⚓

A thick instant. Sometimes the whole train seems to lean. But my bladder was full so I made my way to the toilet at the front end of the café car, stumbling only once into the suited shoulder of a silent, laptop-engrossed businessman. I slid the door shut forcibly once inside, and watched the yellow lock indicator alight.

The feeling arises at the most obvious moments, or the least so: in a commuter-train lavatory, or while on a long airport layover caused by a weather delay, or caught beneath an awning because of a sudden rain, with or without company. Unexpected disruptions in the regular passage of time; moments in which strangers become visible, or intimates become strange. The intuition of an absurdity that can be as little apprehended as it can be flicked away: some solid understanding that overwrites, for an instant, whatever seemed, a moment before, to be so indisputable—so felt—so known. How to name it? "Alive, alive, alive," I sometimes involuntarily whisper, but that isn't the whole story. "Of life" comes closer, though it rings less. Of; a part. No *us* without *them;* no *this* without *me;* no *me* without *you.* Increasingly, an added echo: "despite, despite, despite." I pee, leaning. I get up, shoulder falling to the soft plastic wall. I think of S; even thoughts about not-S are now thoughts of S.

The train rights itself and I unlock the door; the light goes off, indicating something to everyone who sees.

⚓

It was a small difference, but notable—a thing not remarkable in itself, but remarkable for its distinction from the status quo. The conductor, a familiar face, a thirty-something, brown-haired white guy, tall, generic in a way the word seems designed to describe, someone I'd overheard many times detailing to his bored colleagues the circumstances of his divorce ("It was false advertising, you know? She was, like, *mentally ill*."), for the first time swung through the café car to announce that we'd have to vacate it an hour before the train reached its terminus. "Get your things and find a seat in one of the main cars."

We protested. I wasn't the only one who took this train regularly. A college student, grad student, maybe, tattooed and bespectacled, stared up at him: "I've always been able to stay here until my stop." The student's table was strewn with a plugged-in, sticker-covered laptop, an eight-and-a-half-by-eleven reader with a two-inch tape binding, a pair of vintage sunglasses, a tube of hand lotion, a floral-patterned, wax-cloth pencil case. "She has to do inventory," the conductor said. "She's counting thousands of dollars back there. I'm not saying any of you all's going to steal it, but you've gotta find a seat in there. Seven minutes. You're gonna want to pack that stuff up."

⚖

The "stuff" to be packed, in my case, was an old copy of *Astragal,* a gift from my clerk—forgiveness bribe disguised as gift (she'd never shown up to the bar)—left behind the counter with the other clerk, my name printed in blocky red on the brown paper sleeve. *Astragal* was belated, a book I should have found earlier; as soon as I opened it, I resented not having discovered it on my own. And, as soon as I opened it, I knew I would read it, enough of it, and then would send it along to S.

S loved early deaths, and Albertine Sarrazin had one. It wasn't morbid, this attraction, it was—

I've flown away, my dears!

—a tattooed sentence shoves itself into the present, on a slender freckled arm. The student (or grad student, or neither) wants to tell me something; I can't tell what.

"It's from the book you're reading." A finger from the other hand pointing out the sentence, tapping on it. Courier. Courier New, maybe. American Typewriter.

If I were to tell you that within five seconds, this person with the Sarrazin tattoo had fallen into my lap, that my coffee thermos had been thrown onto their lap, which was also my lap, and begun to dribble, and that the conductor, so coolly authoritarian just minutes before, was on the floor crying "Whoa, whoa, whoa!" would you imagine you knew what just happened?

I love it when you try to guess. Sometimes it's exactly what I need.

GASLIGHTS

It was Leslie's idea—the host, and the grower—to screen both versions of the film and to screen them in reverse chronological order, and it was Dawn's idea to make it a potluck, which she organized, making sure that there would be plenty salt, plenty sweet, plenty fat, and plenty crunch. Marc came late, characteristically, but (also characteristically) brought the best booze: a large bottle of hand-labeled medicinal gin. Everybody took off their wet boots, their wet coats, at the door.

You haven't heard these names before, but you know the named: Marc the sweaty hugger from the fair, Leslie the suggester of the composting-toilet syllabus. There was Kim, trailing sawdust from his overalls, and Stella, who'd come straight from the farm. It wasn't clear if the others would show, and we started the film (1944) while circulating a bowl of Gas & Guns.

I sank into the sofa next to Kim, and hesitated when the pipe reached me. I was inexplicably nervous: I could feel my heart pumping, I could hear it in my jaw. I couldn't say what I was anticipating, only that I was anticipating something—and (I can't say how I knew this) that the something had to do with S.

The film's credits sequence, after the MGM lion roars, rolls against a backdrop of stenciled wallpaper and a gaslit sconce—someone said the walls reminded them of a particular image by Bellocq, the one where the photograph's subject is wearing vertically striped stockings and holding a glass up as if for a toast, and someone else said that would make sense since the film is set around the time that photo would have been taken—but it was the score to the credits that got us to sync up our disparate moods: soprano, crash, thud, tremolo, something that could have been a theremin but was probably just violin.

We sank into our positions, sought and found convivial contact (Kim's and my knees touching lightly, unremarked), and readied ourselves to be outraged.

Paula (Ingrid Bergman) is in love: it's ruined her art; it will ruin her life. Of course, we know it—how could we not? We pass the pipe.

No one in the room is in a current relationship, I remember, looking around: divorced; heartbroken; happily single; single and looking; not interested; deep in impossible love.

"Are you afraid?" Gregory asks with his uncanny lisp. "Of me?" "No, of happiness."

"Don't fall for it, Paula!" Marc heckles, uncapping another tonic water drawn from his bag. "Stop spoiling!" Stella whispers, elbowing Marc and making the soda spill.

I'm trying to focus on the film, but the minute the group settles into companionable stillness I leave the scene, as definitively and completely as I remember leaving my bedroom the one night I successfully astral projected—at nineteen or twenty, after studying the technique under Caleb and Mariko all semester, prone on the floor of our shared room in the shared house—and found myself (unoriginally—I'm sorry!) flying over the beleaguered two- and three-story apartment buildings of the surrounding streets, the ungroomed patches of lived-in yard, the late-night stragglers filing out of the every-night live blues spot, and feeling, really feeling, the wind in my face.

I reach for that experience while acknowledging all the ways in which this time is different: I didn't fly; I didn't even leave Leslie's living room, not fully, but it was as if my sensing apparatuses had left the room, had detached themselves both from my material body and from anything that could be figured in language as "my body." And, conversely, while that first time all the drama of the experience was in the mere fact of it—nothing happened other than what I've described: I flew, I viewed my neighborhood from above, I returned—this time, there occurred an event, at least there occurred a part of an event, sadly truncated.

Event is a strong word. What happened was that I encountered— bear with me, that's also not the right word—*sentences*. As if they were creatures, entities (we know they are entities). And the problem is that I can't quote them to you. They're lost; they were too precise to withstand reentry from the dream. I can only paraphrase them, name them, denting them along the way.

There was *Longing #1*, an extended, complex sentence that was really more of a list—there may not have been a verb in it at all, or not an active one—of first encounters (you'll have guessed I experienced all of this in relation to S, somehow, without acknowledging it at the time).

The list is lost to me, though some remnants remain: first touch through clothing; first gesture of removing glasses for an unmediated, reciprocated look (Do I somehow know that S wears glasses? I don't think I do); first tears; first involuntary utterance—"yes"; first confession of desire; but also the lips, the soles of the feet, the asshole, the shadowy region behind the ear.

There was *Rage without Remorse*, which was a political sentence, written in invisible ink—I intuited this somehow. It slid around me like a snake, everywhere it touched became electric. Just describing it now: pinpricks on my right collarbone and under my left breast.

And there was *Longing #2,* an embarrassingly simple sentence that expressed tempered impatience, a particular relation to watching. *Tempered* is not the right word, the relation was less comforting than that. I can't imagine (and this is the point) what *Longing #2's* words were. I return from the sentences abruptly, without warning, to the couch. Kim still beside me, his elbow against my rib. The film on the screen isn't the one we'd been watching when I departed; in my fugue state, I must have missed the changeover to the earlier version (1940). A giant bowl of popcorn has appeared on the coffee table. I reach for a handful; Kim shifts in response, suddenly shy about our sustained contact. The credits roll, and as if we hadn't just been sitting silently for more than three hours, our voices find themselves, and then they find one another again.

No artfully arranged bonfire, no full moon, no escaped longhorn sheep drifting through mist, no mist; no bear cub loping across the road, no heron circling the pond, no exceptionally loud bullfrogs or brilliant fireflies, no inadvertent minimalist or maximalist light-and-sound happening; no illicit undertone, no unexpected guests (desired or not), no dogfights, no dogs; no tears; no conflicts, not exactly, though Leslie and Marc disagree about whether *Gaslight* (1940) or *Gaslight* (1944) is more secretly contemporary, and in their disagreement reveal that their criteria for contemporaneity are similar but their categorical assignments diverge; no music, not outside; not inside, except where the turntable's playing; no news, not anymore, though the day was consumed by it; no senate hearings, no general strike; no talking heads; no Talking Heads, except where the record is spinning for no one; no campfire, except the one we gather around; no love except what we profess; no desperation except what we reject; no moisture except the ground;

no ground; no question, no answer; no morning but for night; no friendship but for benefits; no love but for friends; no fire but for love. Someone found lamp oil when it was needed; no one made a plea for purity; the moon, three-quarters full, gave way to fog; the goats arrived without their horns; the guests were expected. What are we doing circling the fire, not going home?

"List all the things we agree about," says Marc, and by the time we have finished our collaborative account, the returning rain has sent us inside and transformed quickly, from guest to invader, from minimalist to maximalist, from mist to deluge.

THREE

THE NEWS REPORTS
(STRANDED PEOPLE SPREADSHEET)

6 people there and 2 young children, off _____ Trail, _____ Club. Robert _____ is one of them. 15 cabin community off _____ trail?

Off _____ Trail in _____, you take a right off of _____ road which is off of _____. My dad's name is Robert. There are 6

people there and 2 young children, off _____ Trail or road, not sure. 2 young children

not sure. On Rt __, approx. half mile south of _____, small white house with garage, Creekside next to _____ residence,

across from _____ residence. no food, electric, water, phone out, on vacation . . .

the whole crew. my friends and I were able to walk out of _____ today and we met everyone that lives there over the last

few days. Everyone is fine! email me at _____ if you want to find out about specific people. 4 _____ Court. No electric, water. Cat.

Many. _____ Brook Road. Water mess. Limited Electricity. Multiple cats.

37 _____ Rd. They have been seen but they do not have a generator. Obviously no power, etc. They received some dry ice this morning.

At the end of a one-mile-long road. Possible medical, food, water concerns. People are trapped because two bridges are out on Rt __. Elderly, wheelchair-

bound, limited food and water remaining. 1268 _____ Road. Haven't heard from her and don't know if she's o.k. Mary. My mother

may run out of food. _____Road. 2 with med. issues. Not able to connect. 2000_____Valley Road. Lots of people stranded, plenty

of food and a generator. Blocked by ravine though, _____ Road, and bridge out en route to _____. Children.

Resort in _____. Wedding party stranded with no power since Saturday. Road leading to resort washed out. Emergency

responders have gotten through on ATVs. Plenty of food, generator, high spirits.

East branch cut a new bed just to the west of the first bridge on _____ Rd. aka country route __. All people east of the bridge are unable to cross the creek. There is a second location farther east where a smaller creek also tore through.

100+ special-needs campers. They have a generator that has been running the entire time. They are fully staffed

but have been unable to get to town. National Guard told them they hope to have a one-lane "bridge"

by 10:00. Source: my mother-in-law at 39 _____ Road, as well as a neighbor.

As I understand it _____ Road is not passable. Does anyone know when repairs may begin? My 86-yr-old Grandfather is trapped

between _____ Lake and _____ Road. Elderly.

NAMES

ALBERTO
BERYL
CHRIS
DEBBY
ERNESTO

ANDREA
BARRY
CHANTAL
DORIAN
ERIN

ARTHUR
BERTHA
CRISTOBAL
DOLLY
EDOUARD

ANA
BILL
CLAUDETTE
DANNY
ELSA

ALEX
BONNIE
COLIN
DANIELLE
EZEKIEL

POSTCARD FROM S #1
(received upon waking in the afternoon
following the first liveblog night shift)

ALL I WAS THINKING OR WOULD EVER THI NK WAS HAPPENING AND IT COULDN'T BE STOPPED

THE NEWS REPORTS (LIVEBLOG)

Looking for news on _____. Please. Thanks.

Any updates on route 10 North _____, area of _____?

Haven't been able to reach my brother in _____. He has businesses in _____ and _____ Falls. Any news on any of those places?

Does anyone know if route 3 (_____Rd.) is open today, Monday?

We are scheduled to stay at _____ spa tonight. Can't get through to them. Wondering if u have any news? Thank you.

Report from East _____ (near _____): my mom is up there, where she is it's dry but roads blocked around her and no power or water. East _____ fire dept. is out and about. Their phone # appears to be out of service though, so if anyone has a better number please send it to _____. in touch with my mom but it would be good to chat with the guys at the fire house.

Has anyone been up _____ Road in _____? Are the houses up there o.k.?

Thanks for the great job you're doing. We still can't get to our house in _____ County and you've been our best source for updates and links.

Please, can anyone tell me how the area and creeks in the _____ are fairing?

Any info on the South _____ road area of _____?

red cross is fucking useless.

the roads r bad on _____, _____.

I have family members in _____ a half mile from the lower _____. Any news on flooding?

I have friends in _____. Does anyone know anything about that area?

Any news from _____ Lake Road in _____ Center?

My brother, Curt, in _____ is fine. He called his work in _____ and said he hopes to be back Wed. All roads are closed. He was at the _____ campground. I believe he went to the firehouse Sunday a.m.

My parents are in _____ and I can't get through to them. I'm worried. Does anyone have any knowledge of the road conditions there? All the lines appear to be down. Any info would be appreciated!

All true about County Road _____ in East _____. The bridge connecting _____ Rd. to _____ is out, cutting off those people on the road. They all seem to be pulling together, gathering food and finding available propane tanks for communal meals. At the end of the road is the _____ Camp, which apparently has enough food for three days. All of this info gathered from friends on the road. As far as I know, it is not possible to get to _____ or anywhere else from the end of _____ at _____ Road, even if someone could climb down the embankment to get to a car on the other side of the failed bridge. And of course no power there or in any of the surrounding towns.

POSTCARD FROM S #2
(received upon waking in the afternoon following
the second liveblog night shift)

SOME OF US WERE IN THE POND AS THE LEVEL WENT DOWN

THE NEWS REPORTS (FEED)

_____ telecom flooded. says internet will go down soon. liveblog will keep rolling thanks to you all! #ezekiel

Rt. 55 between _____ & _____ is impassable due to downed trees from south _____ road to the 55a intersection.

South _____ Ave. is closed after tree brings down wires. Cones across road. Nobody on the scene. #stranded #ezekiel

All roads closed in _____ County; state of emergency declared. #storm #ezekiel

Reports that the _____ Dam just broke. Waiting to confirm.

News: State of emergency declared in _____, Town of _____, officials declared.

News: Flooding reported in _____ Lake. Lake officials have closed numerous roads. #Recordonline #Ezekiel

News: flooding in _____ Valley area severe and getting worse. Updates.

Trying to get from N___ to _____ville? No dice! #Ezekiel

POSTCARD FROM S #3
(received upon waking in the afternoon following
the third liveblog night shift)

FISH FLUNG ASHORE AND DIED. WE WERE LOVERS AND FRIENDS BUT IT WASN'T ENOUGH

RESPONSE

I wrote S a message, not exactly in response to the postcards but not exactly not in response to them. I wrote, "Dear S, what is the opposite of agoraphobia, I would like to reclaim its literal opposite from its current use, we have so many ways already to describe the love of public fucking, I want a word for love of the marketplace, by which I don't mean the market, I know you understand, can we propose an alternate definition for *agoraphilia* as the love of crowds, specifically the love of the market, agora, not as a site of profit and profiteering, but as a site of mutual admission that any claim to self-sufficiency is a lie?"

I don't know why I strung everything together with commas like that. It felt like a moment of addition, of accrual. Like a moment to reject subordination.

Doesn't matter anyway. The message refused to send.

WHAT WE WEREN'T DOING

while on the night shift or the day shift swatting rumors and con-
firming fears, or while doling out MREs in churches strewn with
sleeping bags and cots, or while standing in waders in basements
wielding buckets while the seismic numbers were revised and various Bodies of Standardized Naming continued to argue—*storm,
hurricane, storm . . .*—what we weren't doing, and it would be
strange to blame us for this (though among the first responders
were some who seemed partial to assigning blame), was paying a lot
of attention to what was happening downriver in the city in which
Love—in another world, it now seemed, though it was the same
world—had met.

The mail still arrived every day, though most of the routes were
interrupted and people had to pick up their letters and parcels at
one of the post offices that hadn't been evacuated. My PO box on
the bottom row in P_____ had been soaked; S's postcards sat in
a regulation cloth sack behind the counter at C_____, where I
had to wait in line for up to an hour to receive them. The last two
arrived on one day, and then for a week there was nothing, and
then I stopped going to the post office in C_____, and then, ten
days after Ezekiel fell, the mail, without warning, stopped coming altogether.

THE NEWS REPORTS

The Glass Bead Game is a book on my shelf. It was given to me by a
girlish boy I called Bambi, with whom I was hopelessly in love. Its
pulverized

cover, green beige with an illegible image, illegible text, is hinge-
taped to the equally pulverized, illegible

spine. I would follow Bambi home on the Tube, pretending I lived
in his neighborhood. I lived

across town, I
read the whole way home, happy in my misery

as now, drunk on disaster, this book
tumbling from the storm-shaken stack.

Once, Bambi almost kissed me, we were high, we'd just finished
our nightly communal theft from the till, café now empty—
almost kissed me, I swear—

later handed me the book, inscribed:
"Take good care of this. It is meaningful tome." Castalia, the
futuristic

site of the novel, gave Tim Leary the name for the rebrand of his
International Federation for Internal Freedom. It's mostly

about men (*The Glass Bead Game*), though there is in a late
chapter a flashback to a time "when women ruled" (this

according to Wikipedia, which also reminded me of aspects of the
plot and characters, including the pagan rainmaker, Knecht,

who, having lost his rain, sacrifices
himself to "the tribe").

It took years for me to realize I'd misread Bambi's loopy
handwriting, to recognize his error

not as grammatical but
calligraphic: the book not

meaningful tome
but *meaningful to me*

which it was

THE MIDDLE PERIOD

I'll leave you here, hand myself over. I know it's sudden, but there are parts of this story that can't be told from the inside. I don't trust myself. (Why should you?)

Who hasn't struggled and failed to tell what matters—political desire, sexual desire, desire for help, desire to help. Intraspecies love, interspecies love. Lost and found and lost, or being-unto-loss: the dagger, suspended above.

The sentiment (a protest) goes something like this: Everyone has lost someone, but *I* have lost someone. Someone loses someone each second, but *I* have lost someone, even this second, and this. The perspective is unconscionably skewed. But still. The dependence of presence on the specter of absence is absurd. When you haven't lost anyone proximally, tragically, the blur edges toward blame, or toward shame.

What can these theories do, in the end? Stories do more, dreams do more.

Theories give shape, in the middle period, to discussions of stories and dreams. Theories help enable interpretations—of stories and of dreams. Interpretations have been useful in the middle period: the period of almost-despair that passes for despair.

By leaving you here, I give myself to story, to dream. By leaving you here, I retain some hope of gathering under their sign. It's late, too; the light is waning and I'm tired.

Signing off, with all my love—

E

FOUR

&

To say that they sat finally together around the rectangular wooden table, battle-worn and unshowered, each clutching a mug of hot cider or a paper cone of boiled and cooled tap water, and that the ones who had come from the city downriver were feeling particularly unmoored while the ones who lived in the village upriver felt the vulnerability of hosts, and that the turn of events that had brought the two groups together, or had at least brought representatives of the two groups together—the turn in which Ezekiel's effects on the village, and to the neighboring towns, had stabilized over the course of a month and then, while everyone was looking the other way, Farrah had arrived to the congested and overbuilt south, stronger than expected and more terribly aimed—to say that all of this was above all *unprecedented*, though also *ironic*, would be to name a situation based on its contours alone, leaving out the mess of particulars without which the contours would have nothing to contain.

To say that this is a story, finally, of two inquiries or conversations, two types or typologies, two interlocking hands, would be to tell the part of the story that can be told in this way while leaving out the part that can be told only by slowing down time, or by stopping it—long enough for the shock of misfortune to fade and for the people around the table (readers and syllabus-makers all, you remember, and as a consequence accustomed to one way in which time gets rearranged) to stop sorting each other into sides: Love, Anti-.

To say that E sat at the head of the table and S at the foot would be to forget that the reverse was equally true—no matter. What matters is that they faced each other for the first time in public, after the months of serious play and playful seriousness, after the postcards and the dreams (lucid and otherwise), now beneath the cloud of a set of circumstances they could no more control than they could have created them, that they could no more ignore than they could swat them away with a totemic book from one of their overlapping lists.

"Loves," said E, then took a sip from her mug. "Comrades." She put the mug down. "Let's everyone introduce ourselves."

&

But before this, before the table and the assembly around it, there
has to be the first time.

There was always going to be a first time. E knows this; you know
it. S knew it, though we don't have much access to S, not yet, which
means we don't yet know what knowing feels like for S. This is, of
course, always the case—the not-knowing, the lack of access, the
delay, or what we kid ourselves is a delay but what is, more accu-
rately or at least much more commonly, an infinite deferral. "You
can't know what I feel," said the husband, back in Part One (offstage; not everything gets written down). "But I have to tell you
anyway, and your job is to suffer from the not-knowing, as I have
suffered, am suffering, from the feeling."

This isn't the way the husband talked, you understand. Not in the
mediation sessions, and not in the part of his life he called "real."
Often the husband didn't talk at all, but he was possessed with
an uncommon talent for communicating without words: sentences
such as the above would be contained and conveyed within a routine
activity that involved an intricate series of small motions—making
a coffee with the stove-top espresso pot, for example—voiced only
by the endemic sounds of those motions, along with an occasional
sigh or an extraneous clearing of the throat. By the time the funnel
filter was emptied with a single knock against the metal trash can;
by the time the stove had been lit with a match and the faucet run
to clean the rubber gasket and the stainless-steel filter plate and to
fill the lower body of the carafe with water; by the time the boiling

coffee had burbled up through the stem and into the upper body, a mug had been retrieved from the cupboard with the creaky hinge, half-and-half pulled from the droning fridge and stirred into the mug with the back end of a butter knife wrested from the clattering, overfull dish drainer, the sum total of the sounds and their instigating movements would convey, wordlessly, the husband's claim.

If you remember from Part One, E, acting as our narrator, dispensed suddenly, unceremoniously, with the husband and the wife, or with E's speculations, which is all they were, about the husband and the wife. The wife, regular witness and audience to dramas like the coffee-making scene above, was no more an avatar for E than was the husband himself, but both made E uncomfortable, and she shoved them off, a by-product of her mentor's disappearance. Now, with the *first time* approaching just as quickly or slowly as the beleaguered and unpredictable thruway was moving the afternoon before the day on which S and the others were slated to show up in the place where Anti-Love met, E found herself thinking again about the husband and the wife, about how she'd more or less abandoned them and about what had happened offstage that might be relevant to her now.

She was about to lay her eyes on S, and that meant that something was going to happen to her expectations, because something always happens to expectations when time and opportunity force them out of hiding.

She had no rulebook; she had only the disappearing clerk, some others before and since, and the husband and the wife—failed experiments all—to turn to for context and preparation.

This is where we have arrived.

E is about to lay her eyes on S: a first that might be a last, or that might be one of a series of firsts. She has no way to prepare, so she makes a stove-top espresso and listens—knock, strike, rinse, fill, hum, clatter—for the sentence that will tell her what she doesn't know she knows.

&

No sentence came, nor was there time for one to form; before she brought the coffee mug to her lips, a shadow fell on the kitchen floor, interrupting the stream of morning sun, and a knock turned her around to face the slatted-glass door as she heard the sounds of a car reversing out of her gravel drive.

The sun was streaming directly through the glass so she couldn't see the face of the standing figure; the next thing she knew the door was pushed in, and an enormous wirehaired dog barreled into E's thighs, whinnying.

It was easier not to look up at S. It was easier to face the dog: a buck-toothed, wild-eyed, brindle mix of who knows what breeds. An unimaginable dog, just as S had been—and remained, for seconds longer, or as long as E could delay—unimaginable.

"That's Splice," a voice said, and E gave in to the polite obligation to look up.

As she did, the mass of coarse brindle hair launched toward her face, preceded by a giant pinkish tongue.

"Splice, so happy to meet you," E laughed, subconsciously assessing the dog's potential for craziness before performing the bonding gesture she had made, since she was a child, with every dog whose craziness potential was low: she boxed Splice's ears with her hands and brought its forehead to meet hers, then, through a series of deliberate inhalations and exhalations, synchronized their breathing. This, of course, though it was a genuine and longstanding habit, at the moment served mostly to put off facing S for as long as the situation would allow.

&

E's house, the house she rented from the last surviving offspring of a family that had been in the area for many generations, twin sisters who had both moved to a retirement home in Orlando and relied on the modest rent from E to supplement their social security payments and other fixed income (in one case an inheritance from a dead husband, and in the other a school librarian's pension—E had gleaned all of this from the one conversation the three women had when the lease was signed), was once a trailer.

The trailer had been added on to over the years, always illegally and only semicompetently (mostly by the sisters themselves), with one new "wing" appended to the side and another "master suite" off the back; at some point the whole collage, with its uneven ceiling height and incoherent window placement, had been covered in a skin of vinyl siding so that, from the outside, it looked almost convincingly like an actual house—a single wide with a generic addition, like many of the other houses on the steep, semipaved, sparsely populated road. The one thing that distinguished E's house from the others was its front door, which was the original 1960's trailer door: narrow; red-and-white metal; with wide, movable horizontal slats stacked from top to bottom—an original, hard-to-replace jalousie door, she'd been told by the twins.

"Cool door," S said as E finally straightened up to stand.

As E stood, she kept her head pointed down to the floor, cheap parquet laid on top of some toxic subfloor she preferred not to wonder about. This wasn't voluntary—she felt as if someone very heavy, some giant, were pressing down on the nape of her neck, tilting her head forward like a hairdresser who doesn't know their own strength. As she stood, she could feel the approach of S's face; meanwhile, Splice wedged its head between E's legs, just above the knees.

S was still, they both were silent.

E realized she'd closed her eyes and now she opened them, stared down at Splice's chaotic mane, positioned between her blue-jeaned legs and S's corduroyed ones. She lifted her eyes without shifting the position of her head: a torso behind a T-shirt behind an open, worn-out wool coat. Lifting her hands to touch it was like lifting her feet from the mud in the dream she'd had (old house, mossy pool), which now came to mind with such disorienting force she got lightheaded and nearly fell.

She placed her hands on S's ribs, both palms flat against the T-shirt, edging under the musty coat. By the time she looked up, it wouldn't have mattered what she saw.

&

Two hours later, after more coffee had been made and consumed, after the dog had been settled into a makeshift bed of old blankets, the postcards acknowledged but not explained, and the stacks of books on the coffee table and on the floor lightly browsed and casually rearranged; after the two bodies had noticed without comment their near-identical size and weight, their symmetrical arms and kindred hair, their wardrobe similarities and their identically groomed nails; after each had put a hand down the other's pants; after one had brought the other's finger up and bitten it, hard; after the woodstove had been stoked and eggs had been scrambled and devoured, E looked across the table at S. "I can't figure out what you look like," she said. "I can see you, but I can't picture you. What's that about?" And S said, "It's o.k., I don't need to be pictured. There are other things I need." And the sun emerged from behind a cloud and they decided to take the dog out for a walk.

Some facts may have been misrepresented, or misleadingly described.

The mail did cease to arrive, but only for two days. It was unprecedented, but then quickly normalized into a glitch. The post office issued a terse statement arguing, in effect, that they'd had a pretty good run of *neither snow nor rain nor heat nor gloom of night* and that, with the budget cuts, the dominance of internet communication, increased competition from private carriers, and the declining health of their aging workforce (the number of postal workers shot or killed by dogs had doubled annually for the last five years; the young underemployed couldn't be enticed to join), they would continue to reserve the right to pause service in localized areas when acts of God rendered delivery *virtually impossible.*

There is a version of this story in which the city where Love once met—the city in which the apartment across from the café, the bodega, and the playground is situated—is underwater, in chaos, a battleground or a breeding ground or a mass grave. You wanted a story, and that would have been a good one, ripe with analogies to our present age, rich with interpretables, a litmus test for those who read it, distributing them (whether or not they were aware that their deepest responses to the narrative, the ones that protest or agree with a character's reaction to a situation of threat, distribute them thus) along the temperamental continuum from *stasis-preserving* to *experimental,* the reformers and the burners-to-the-ground. It would have helped us, perhaps, imagine the actual future for which we are more or less bound, though without knowing when.

But that isn't what's happened, what's happening here.

If this is a News Report, it must mention a book, and if it must mention a book, it should be *The Desert*—a poetry, a research, picked up by E and S from the stack that first night and read aloud to each other, rapt—

> *People are snakes*
> *Swimming only*
> *To keep moving*

—and to which we may, explicitly or not, return—

/ end of Report

&

They were city people, S and E. This doesn't mean the same thing to everyone, but it seemed to mean something similar to S and E: that they recognized they had been formed by grids and laws and the application of power to land; by climate control and light control and the anarchic organization of pedestrian life; by streets named for digits, politicians, artists, and states; by bars spilling into streets and the other way around; by the beautiful violence of millions of bodies navigating daily proximity; by the moments of excess—blackouts, heat waves—when difference fleetingly recedes; by the moments when instead it gets cruelly amplified; by the minute calculations needed to balance witnessing, action, and survival; by implication and exploitation more generally.

They were also linked by their exposure—S's irregular but long-standing, E's increasingly committed and durational—to the non-city and to what it had begun to teach them: about seasons, about autonomy, about vulnerability, about collaboration, about time.

In this moment, they were city people or former city people walking a dog through fields of flagging goldenrod, expired late-season blackberries, yellowing birch and reddening maple trees. They pointed at things and named them when they could: lion's mane, self-heal. Splice ran after a rabbit and nosed some bear scat. They came upon a dead rabbit and had to drag the dog away.

☙

Recognizing things did not mean understanding them, and this was why S and E's first in-person conversation consisted almost entirely of questions answered by questions.

S: Do you think time will ever feel the way it did before the internet?

E [laughs]: Do you think I'll ever finish reading another book?

S: What if I write one for you?

E: How long will it be?

S: What's the right length?

E: Haven't you noticed that all the books in my piles have bookmarks between pages twenty-five and one hundred?

S: Haven't you noticed that there's a lot for me to notice right now?

E: What if I write one for you?

S: What if I hold you to that?

Splice barreled down the hill from behind E and S, having made the loop around the field without them, and plowed between their legs, then skidded to a stop, turned, and waited, wagging, for them to show their love.

A LONG NIGHT

In the kitchen, Splice lapping at its water bowl, E and S turned serious. First about eating—the early fall of night had made them hungry—and then about coffee.

S joked about the fancy coffee grinder and E self-incriminated— "I'm part bourgeois, never said I wasn't"—which prompted E to tell S in detail about the imagined playground scene with the capitalist, which prompted S to tell E about a hundred tiny similar scenes, some true and some only fantasized, which prompted E to tell S about the long-ago sessions with the bookstore clerk with the cherry-red lips, which prompted S to say to E, "I feel strangely at home in your presence," to which E responded, "I know what you mean."

And with that, so many questions and expectations fell away— the anarchist of anti-Science would approve—that S and E began to feel, each in their own way, which they took turns describing to each other, the appearance of a clearing or a field (whether it was the same field or two separate fields, they didn't wonder at) into which appeared, or began to appear, *figures,* leftovers or remainders, ruins, like the undone architecture and spent debris that persisted on the sites of the houses in the town neighboring E's, the place Ezekiel had injured most.

"What are these figures?" S asked E, stroking E's arm on the downbeat of each word.

"I don't know what they are," said E. "Let's count them. That at least will give us something sure."

They closed their eyes and counted. An observer would think their lives depended on it: wrinkled brows, puckered lips, eyes roving behind their lids.

Then they opened their eyes at the same moment, smiled, and opened their mouths. "Twenty-seven," they said in unison, and Splice barked at the post-silence noise.

⚬

"Twenty-seven *whats*?" said E.

[Pause]

"Twenty-seven Figures of Concern," said S, fake-serious (but also serious).

"What should we do with them?" said E.

"We should address them."

FIRST FIGURE

S: This one I see clearly, like a line drawing that is somehow also three dimensional. It might be a mountain, or a nipple, or a wart, or the nose on the face of a person lying on the beach and staring at the sky. The strange thing is how I can feel, in real time, right now, how that list of associations reduces to two, and how those two reduce to a challenge in scale and in perspective. Nose. Mountain. Nose. Mountain. Whose nose is it? Whose mountain? I look out your window and I see: a mountain. What mountain is that?

[At this, S turned to face E, causing a replay of the first shock of recognition: an aftershock. E felt S's gaze but didn't meet it, looked instead out at the mountain.]

E: It must have many names, but the internet calls it Johnson's Nose.

SECOND FIGURE

E: This one feels like a Rorschach test; it makes me anxious. I recognize two logical symbols, greater than and less than, facing each other. (Why is it so hard to resist anthropomorphizing everything—it's just a couple of lines bent at angles and symmetrically arrayed!) I wonder if it would be different if the lines felt machine-made, if they were straight, perfectly measured. If this were an artwork, I'd give it multiple titles.

S: Tell me some of them.

E [without hesitation]: "Detranslation," "Kinds of X," "A Match," "Let Me Tell You a Story about Your Life," "Inflection Point," "Choice or No," "Participation," "Get Here Now."

THIRD FIGURE

S: They seem to want us to move quickly from one to the next, but do you notice how the first and second figures have faded and are disappearing? As if our descriptions fulfill their being, as if our address is mortal. This one implicates me, I can feel it, but I can't tell why. The flourish in the center, that curl, feels both decorative and necessary: if the figure is a path, the curl is a detour, making the line a flaneur. I stand silenced.

E [after a pause]: Do you see yourself as a flaneur? What does that mean to you?

S: I waste time. I'm happiest when I'm being unproductive. The guilt I feel for this is a guilt I disavow, but disavowal is not enough to make it go away. Let me try again to explain what I mean. I've written to you already of my obsession with eavesdropping, and of my inability to strategize. That curl in the middle of this figure? It's my happy place.

FOURTH FIGURE

E: A boat! With a fucked-up sail. And a fucked-up shape. And no mast, and no crew, and no flag. No way could this boat sail. We'd be playing cards below, canasta or Omaha or Oh Hell! We'd be so caught up in it all, a little drunk or high but only enough for time to get screwy, sitting across from each other at the built-in wood table with its marine-grade varnish, vaguely aware of our reflections in it, or else trying to use the reflection to cheat . . . We'd be so engrossed in either the game or the conversation or the ambient hum of the boat's cavity—our common heart—we wouldn't notice as the water level out the porthole windows crept slowly up. It wouldn't be a dramatic death, we'd just drop silently, incrementally, to the bottom together, and stop being alive without really dying.

[E put her hand to her mouth and looked up to the nighttime kitchen window, at S's reflection, which was waiting there to meet E's eyes.]

E: Isn't it crazy what can happen outside time?

FIFTH FIGURE

[Before addressing the fifth figure, S and E wordlessly negotiated a move to the adjacent room: rug, floor cushions, stacks of books, coffee table, bottle of Mexican dark rum, in one corner of the floor a tangle of miniature amber holiday lights set in a large bowl; S poured two glasses of rum, and E plugged in the lights. The field of figures, naturally, moved with them.]

S: This one makes me laugh. But maybe I'm just relieved that dying in the fourth figure didn't mean actually dying in your kitchen. I wonder why this one makes me laugh? It's just an L, or a chair, or a bend in the road.

E: It's that tail, the little thing at the end, isn't it? Like a drip, or like ejaculate. Excess. It's funny because it's too much.

S: A directional change that turned out to be a miscalculation. Overconfident navigation! The feeling of laughter is leaving me. Now I'm sensing a kind of terror. Now all I can think of is the word *precipice*. Help me think of another word.

E [reaching for S's hand]: I'm so sorry. Nothing comes to mind.

SIXTH FIGURE

E [after a silence, bashfully]: This one reveals the fact that I'm not an artist—if I could draw, I would not be able to see what I see, which is a shard, specifically a glass shard from a shattered drinking glass—like this one.

[E held up her glass and turned it in her hand, trying to force the figure to conform to the shape of a fragment that might break off from its rim.]

S: Drawing is easy, you know, it's just a mind trick. You have to use your eyes and not your brain. You have to connect your eyes to your hand directly.

[S lifted a hand, index finger extended, to trace E's sternum slowly from top to bottom.]

E: I've followed that instruction before and produced passable results. Still lifes. Charcoal nudes. But they aren't alive. They're like singing in someone else's voice.

S: Why do you think you're seeing a shard, even though you're seeing something that's hard for you to picture as a shard?

E: Maybe any figure I addressed in this moment would find a way to remind me of this thing I've been wanting to say, about injury, about what they call "grit." But the moment's passed now. I'm no longer in the mood.

SEVENTH FIGURE

S: Let's do this easy one then. Look at that shape, it's obviously a house.

E: And yet, I never lived in a house that looked like that. Until, I guess [E looked around] maybe this one.

The field, which had been filling the room with its figures almost to the extent that the room had receded into a sketch of itself—as if the field, which was imagery, and the house, which was material, had swapped ontological roles—now allowed itself to be outshone by the living room's interior, which meant that the interior, its rug and cushions, stack of books, and tangle of miniature lights, but also its narrow upright shelving, its three framed pieces of art and one unframed poster tacked up with pins, its faded floral curtains and its gloss-painted door, became itself again, but did so anxiously, unreassuringly, less (E thought) like the return to sepia Kansas in *The Wizard of Oz* than like the perilous sunlit past in *Bonjour Tristesse*. The field almost immediately reclaimed its prominence, as if to remind E and S—if they needed reminding—that reality was playing out in the field now. That the field is the room.

EIGHTH FIGURE

E: Well, this one's easy. If that was a house, this is a broken home: with a hole in the roof like that, what kind of protection can it provide?

S: Well, I never experienced my home as protection.

S downed the glass of rum and poured another; E kept her distance with everything but her eyes. When she spoke, she invited S to elaborate, and after a moment of hesitation, S did.

NINTH FIGURE

E: This one reminds me of what just happened. It's a tongue, and it's also an eye. The tongue is yours, telling me about your childhood just now. The eye is mine, a focusing machine, and a factory of tears.

S: I don't mind that you cried. You're a crier. It's one of the differences between us, I'm starting to understand.

E: I've never been embarrassed about being a crier. Though there have been times when it's been used against me.

TENTH FIGURE

E: Do you want some more food? This one made me think about hunger. What I mean is that it made me think about how much I want an avocado. And given where we are and the state of the supermarket shelves, we're a long way from the nearest avocado.

S [letting out a laugh that set Splice to barking again]: It's funny the kinds of things we don't know about each other. I can't eat avocados. I'm allergic. But let's get a snack. Splice wants to go out. Let's go look at the stars—the field and its figures will be here when we get back.

ELEVENTH, TWELFTH, AND THIRTEENTH FIGURES

S [settling back down on one of the big cushions, hands wrapped around a mug of tea]: I don't know if it's because we were out looking at stars, maybe I'm seeing an afterimage, but do those three dots seem to you to be in motion? Moving toward each other, finding each other from different parts of the field.

E: When I worked in magazines, my first job consisted mainly of replacing the triple periods writers would put into their sentences to function as ellipses with the character for an ellipsis—the old programs didn't do that automatically. I always thought it was weird how a full stop, repeated three times, became transformed into an indicator of gap or suspension. Like the too-muchness of all the certainty had the reverse effect: too much presence equals absence. But now I'm seeing something else in this figure, the head of a nail, times three. I'm imagining hammering a nail into a coffin (something I've never, by the way, done). And then hammering again, and then again. And the coffin becoming less solid, instead of more so. The coffin, on the third strike, falling apart.

S: Do you mean literally or figuratively?

E: What?

S: The thing about the coffin and the nail and what you've never done.

FOURTEENTH FIGURE

S: Well, that's just the sign for Aquarius.

E: It is?

[S gave E a disbelieving look.]

E: No, really, it just looks like a zigzag to me.

FIFTEENTH FIGURE

E: Oh! Pillow.

S: Oh, pillow . . . Are you tired?

E: My cells are vibrating, and yet I feel like I'm already asleep. You?

SIXTEENTH FIGURE

E [as S sleeps]: I have no one to address but you directly, now, figure number sixteen, you oblong, egg-shaped thing. You must be
the problem I have to face alone. You must be what I meant when I
asked, before, whether it was possible to love someone who doesn't
share your wounds. Someone with different wounds. Nobody has
escaped being wounded altogether. This was what I almost spoke
to S about, before, when I mentioned something about the glass
shards, about grit. About how . . .

SEVENTEENTH FIGURE

S [as E sleeps]: Well, that's just not fair, you aren't even a figure.
What are you, a line? o.k., a line.

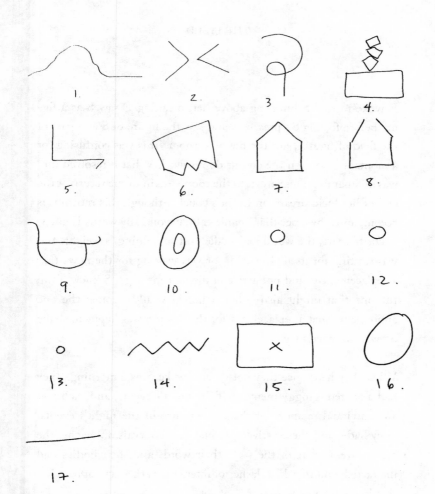

1.

2.

3.

4.

5.

6.

7.

8.

9.

10.

11.

12.

13.

14.

15.

16.

17.

THE FIELD

E woke to find S hovering above her, meaning E saw S as a figure before feeling S's presence, and saw the figure of S as a part of the field of figures, not the material room. This was confusing for a moment, and then the confusion resolved. What it resolved into was an unambiguous return to the room—akin to the return at the end of her lucid dream on Leslie's couch—though this return was accompanied by a peculiar, manic calm beyond any words E knew.

For S's part, the world had shaken off something, a weight, and was waiting for its replacement, or was waiting for the news that a replacement would not arrive (a distinct message, S knew, from the one that might also—that S hoped would—come: the one announcing that a replacement for the thing S was happy to shake off was not necessary).

What they had, once they both were awake, was a morning. They had a shared, groggy memory of the night's events, and each had an individual memory of their experience of the night's events. They had—and these arrived gradually, at intervals, for each—the somatic reminders of the ways their words and their bodies had interacted, and they had flashes of interactions they'd imagined but that had not come to pass, or not yet.

They had coffee, and oatmeal, and a long walk with Splice, up the road and into an unknown neighbor's field, where the dog feasted on smells and the occasional pile of deer shit S and E were walking too languorously to avoid.

As they walked, they were mostly silent. At one point S reminded E of an early-hours moment of misunderstanding, and E reassured S that any damage done had been repaired. At one point E asked S, "Do you think we're more alike or more different?" and S laughed and said, "We're really alike," and then, "We're really different," and E said, "Do you think we'll go back to the field again?" and S said, "We only got as far as figure seventeen—of twenty-seven," and E said, "I don't remember the other ten," and S said, "If they want to bring us back, they'll bring us back."

⚬

"This is ridiculous," E said, flashing her version of anger, her face hot in the still-cool air. "People don't pair-bond in a single night, like birds." S gave her a look. "I know 'birds' is not a very specific category. And I don't know how long it takes for them to pair. But what I mean is, neither of us is looking for that, right?"

"Splice!" S yelled, and the dog froze in the field as a pickup truck shot past behind them on the dirt road.

"Let's go in," S said, when the dust had dispersed. "We've got the meeting this afternoon. I'll need coffee first."

FIVE

AN ORIENTATION

Pablo has a bad sense of direction. Or he has a bad sense of orientation, or a good sense of disorientation. Whatever you call it, Pablo
hides it well.

It isn't that he doesn't know where he has found himself, after
the circuitous ride on the volunteer bus, through increasingly less
familiar two-lane highways and cliffside roads. They have passed
by dozens of similarly disused compounds—clusters of small
dwellings, cabins or sheds, the occasional yurt—some with half-
defoliated vines spilling from their paneless windows, a preview for
the arriving season's show. None of the compounds seemed occupied, but Pablo knew they may be; he had been an invisible resident
more than once in his life. People are easy to fool.

Now, alone at the white plastic folding table, a paper cup of cold
coffee in front of him and a paper plate of peanut-butter cookies
to his side, beneath the canvas roof of a canvas tent insufficiently
heated by three upright propane torches, he buttoned up his jacket
and pulled a notebook from its pocket. His ambivalence about
where he'd landed was almost too much to bear. At least he would
record the day's events.

ANOTHER ORIENTATION

The woman with the short silver hair—"my brief haircut," she had taken to calling it, since she gave it to herself every few days with a pair of manual clippers she carried in her bag; the whole operation took less than ten minutes—tilted her head away from the morning sun she'd paused to take in full-face, opened her eyes, and saw, down the path, the canvas tent she'd been expecting. She glanced again at the note in her hand: *If you see the translator, make friends. He might let you share his table.*

On the tent's aluminum-frame door was a small paper sign legible only from a close distance, typed in all caps on a manual typewriter: PERSONAL REPAIR CAFÉ. The silver-haired woman put the note back in her bag, alongside the clippers and an unbound photocopy of the Manual, and turned the handle.

To say, as E did once, that Pablo left *because he was needed* was a kind of shorthand, a bluff. To say *It wasn't that he didn't know where he'd found himself* was also shorthand: he had been told where he was—he'd also read the sign on the door, coming in—but his role there was unclear. He knew, or rather he sensed, that his job, if it could be described as a job, would have something to do with translation, but that was it.

The mentor, on that furtive call, had reminded E of the Manual because she, the mentor, had worked hard on it and because E was, of all her students, the one who had most astutely and productively questioned its techniques. It was the self-confidence apparent in E's judgment (the self-confidence of a person who self-identified as lacking confidence, as lacking, at times, *self*) that impressed and reassured the mentor, both about E and about the Manual's ulti-mate value. The Manual was not meant to be followed obediently; its title and authoritative appearance were a recruiting trick.

⚓

There was no one in the dark tent; at least, it had the feeling of vacancy; the mentor stood by the door and let her eyes adjust. White plastic folding tables lined the edges of the provisional room. She noted the plywood platform the tent was constructed on: a semi-permanent structure, and not a new one. Faded curved and colored lines were visible on the plywood, which, without knowing much about team sports, the mentor took to be related to one or more of them: basketball, dodgeball, who knows what else.

Only after her eyes had fully adjusted, had swept halfway around the tent in a clockwise direction, taking in not only the sequence of tables but their various offerings (not all of them, or hardly any of them, recognizable, but which included sewing machines, small hydraulic pumps, stacks of books, piles of wrenches and other hand tools, and, distributed among them, unidentifiable forms or fig-ures apparently made from terra-cotta, some on tables and some on the floor), did she see, at the farthest table from where she stood, a seated person, sipping something from a paper cup.

"Hello!" said the mentor, walking briskly across the floor. "I'm Marina. I'm looking for the translator."

"I'm the translator," said Pablo. "Pablo."

They shook hands.

"Cookie?"

⚘

Marina and Pablo ate peanut-butter cookies and looked around. They each, in turn, considered speaking, opening their mouths, and then reconsidered, realizing they didn't yet know what to say. The sun moved into a direct shot of the sheet-plastic windows cut through the tent's long sidewall, and the increased brightness made the array of tools and strewn-about terra-cotta figures ever more chaotic and absurd. They chewed their cookies and swallowed, opened their mouths to speak, closed them again. Went back for more cookies. Finally, simultaneously, they burst out laughing.

"What the fuck," said Pablo.

"*is* this place?" said Marina.

A DRIVE

E was silent for the first half of the drive; S sat pensively in the passenger seat, humming in a soft, low voice.

"Do you think," S said, and then stopped. The car was alone on the two-lane county highway, threading through fields and past trailers, cabins, old farmhouses. S's hand was on E's knee.

"Do I think?" E answered, keeping her eyes on the road, slowing down for a deer.

"Do you think a psychological orientation to the world and a political orientation to the world are always at odds? I mean, are they mutually exclusive? Or are they always both present, but in different proportions, so the painful part about sorting them out is that, at the end of the day, you still have to pick one?"

"Do you?"

"Do you what?"

"Have to pick one?"

S was silent now, forgetting even to hum.

"I think you do. In the sense that, like, if you don't eat meat and it's the end of the world and the only thing you can find to eat is a squirrel, then you have to either eat the squirrel or not eat the squirrel. You can't both eat and not eat the squirrel. You have to eat the squirrel or die."

"Does it have to be a squirrel?" E was laughing.

"I don't know if you're allowed to make fun of me yet." S was also laughing but was no longer touching E's knee.

"I don't see the analogy exactly, I mean, the squirrel thing," E said. "But I think I'm following what you mean. Soft psychology, hard politics, soft feeling, hard ideology, right? But isn't it a false binary? If politics is relational, then who's relating? Psychologies. Am I too simple, to be getting stuck there? Because I do."

E had to bring the car nearly to a stop to let a family of turkeys cross.

"Why did you invite us all to come up here?" S said.

E turned to S. "All I did was post the address to the list."

"Maybe we're both too simple," S said, as E pressed on the gas.

ASPECTS OF QUESTIONING

Pablo had stepped out, and now that Marina was alone, she was overcome with a sense of unease. What the fuck was this place, really? It was one thing to voice the question with Pablo, who, while still a stranger, was comfortably legible to Marina as a type: translators, interpreters, mediators, therapists, negotiators—it was easy to recognize something familiar, a common practice if not a common approach or methodological orientation (the intensity of ideological battles within these fields was in fact a testament to that mutual recognition, which Marina always felt had something to do with listening, or at least with a desire to be listening).

Not knowing what to do with her hands—she hadn't known what to do with her hands since she quit smoking fifteen years ago—she pulled out the Manual and opened it at random to a page titled "Aspects of Questioning." She ran her finger down the page. Marina always read equally with her hand and her ear, sometimes also with her mouth, voicing the words at a low volume. But this time it was enough to feel the words as she pronounced them in her head. She was aware of the cliché as it came to her, that the words—not this particular arrangement of them, but words in general—felt like friends.

She read through the taxonomy she had created, in conjunction with her own mentor and with subsequent collaborators over the years:

Aspects of Questioning

Open-Ended Questions ("Please tell me more about what happened.")

Questions to Discover Feelings ("How did you feel when that happened?")

Questions to Learn More about Underlying Issues

Questions Related to "Offers" Made by the Participants ("You said you would be willing to wash the paint off her locker, is that correct?")

"What If?" Questions

Some Useful Questions for Building a Future Story ("What do you want to see happen?" "How do you think this could be resolved?" "What would you be willing to do?")

SIGNS

Pablo's tobacco supply was low. He reached into the plaid, wax-lined pouch and pulled out a smaller clump than usual, enough to roll the thinnest cigarette that would still be enjoyable to smoke. He'd run out of filters already and was secretly enjoying the excuse not to use one while recognizing that he was under no illusion that the filters offered real protection for his lungs. He lit the cigarette and took a long drag, exhaled and looked back at the tent some thirty feet away from where he now stood, in a gravel patch next to a rusted barbecue grill. He was happy for Marina's company, but he'd needed suddenly to get outside, to see if he could get his bearings from an exterior view. To remember what bearings felt like.

The sun continued to strengthen and he unbuttoned his jacket, closed his eyes, and faced the bright heat until the scene behind his eyelids was gradually flooded—from the edges inward—with a deep fuchsia, a brighter magenta spot in its hot center, and the muscles around his eyes began to quiver from the effort of squinting.

He opened his eyes, found a stump to sit on, and reached into his bag for a book.

Marina sat behind the table, continuing to flip through the Manual as the door opened and people began to file in and take their stations behind the other tables, unpacking bags and backpacks and neatening or continuing to set up their displays. She noticed them taking no notice of her; she wondered if she had been rendered invisible by backlighting, the way Pablo had been when she first entered the tent, or whether this was one of those forms of gathering where people assume familiarity with their roles because of the roles' formality: you are sitting behind the desk, so you must be the receptionist; you are the one behind the DJ booth; you are the one collecting donations while playing the violin. Marina's least favorite thing was to engage in those kinds of automatic and unspoken assignations, which is one reason she had gravitated toward mediation, where the airing out of unspoken relation is a large part of the task at hand. (It was not redundant or mere politeness, in Marina's view, to walk into a room in which only a mediator is expected and to say, "Hello, I'm the mediator." It was a small but potentially transformative act.)

But Marina's favorite thing was to be in a place where, because she actually and honestly did not know where she was or why, taking a role either implicitly or explicitly became impossible. Those places, those situations, were hard to come by, but she was beginning to think that she may have landed in one.

The book—more a pamphlet or zine, a staple-bound thing on saturated blue-on-cream paper that he couldn't remember acquiring until he recalled barely seeing it slipped into his bag by E's friend (let's call her Z) on the day she left him suddenly, stating without rancor that his level and kind of devotion weren't enough. "Some people are born for loyalty and some for autonomy," Z had offered as a reason—the way a person quotes scripture or the twelve steps, he'd thought with something less than generosity—"and we are not on the same side of that divide."

It was a collection of images photographed in Thailand by a traveling artist, pictures of signs posted to trees. It was unclear to Pablo whether the images were photographic collages or undoctored found scenes, and whether, if undoctored, they were documentation of an art installation or of a cultural phenomenon.

Because Pablo was Pablo, he also wondered whether there was a difference between these things.

The signs were all bilingual; English text, presumably translations, printed beneath the Thai read "The entire world revolves in your mind" and "To do good and evil unseen by others is always seen by oneself" and "Crying with the wise is better than laughing with the fool" and "Everyone may be a fool but nobody is a fool forever" and—possibly his favorite (Pablo felt, rightly or wrongly, that as a translator he had a special dispensation to appreciate translation "errors" for their poetry)—"Please be aware of your belonging."

When he looked up from the book, a stream of people was flowing into the tent.

Her invisibility seemingly intact, Marina sat still and looked around the room at the newcomers. Each was engaged in a series of movements that appeared to be so rehearsed as to be unconscious—she thought of the choreography of the assembly line in *Modern Times*, the way the Chaplin character's job—tightening bolts—becomes so automatic that everything of a certain size and shape becomes a bolt to be tightened.

She now noticed that each of the newcomers—the incoming stream had stopped already—included as part of their choreography the act of hanging out an identifying sign in front of their tables. Some of the signs Marina was able, at least partially, to read.

"Division of Electrical and Synaptic Repair," one advertised. "Division of the Worn _____," read another, its rightmost edge obscured by a reflective flare of light. There were also "Division of Muted Expectations," "Division of Phantom Cure" (or "Phantom Care," she wasn't sure), "Division of Cleaning the Twelfth House," "Division of ___sibility," and "Division of the Irrevocably Mechanical."

She counted eleven tables other than her own; it occurred to her that she and Pablo might also be expected to put out signs, but then she had the idea to walk around to the front of her table to take a look and saw that a sign had already been affixed to the front of her half of the table—it read "Division of Conflict"—and another to the front of Pablo's half that read "Division of Conversation."

The sign on the door had changed. It was the same sign, but the words on it had changed. Pablo was certain it had read PERSONAL REPAIR CAFÉ when he arrived—he and Marina had even wondered aloud together at the wording and its meaning. Now, in the same manual typewriter font on the same (it seemed) rectangle of paper, the sign read SELF REPAIR CAGE.

He tossed his extinguished cigarette to the ground and went back in.

THE ENTIRE WORLD REVOLVES IN YOUR MIND

Here's the thing. Remember when E was on the train and everything lurched? And then she went into the train's bathroom—or maybe first she went into the bathroom, and then everything lurched, the order doesn't really matter—and she tried to describe what it felt like to be overcome, without warning or explanation, by a feeling of being especially (she would cringe at this description, though the word is hers) *alive?*

The entire world revolves in your mind. A fact, described as simply as description will allow, as translation will facilitate. People who understand anxiety or depression—E and S firsthand, but also the analyst from Anti-Love—know that this is a truism that is also a trap.

When Pablo was told by E's friend Z, by way of breaking things off with him for good, that some people are raised for loyalty and some for autonomy, Pablo's heart rate rose. "That is a false dichotomy!" he protested, and he believed in his protest wholeheartedly (which, for Pablo, who could be a gadfly even to himself, was not always the case). The truth was, he did not want to be forced to choose which type of person he was—any more than E, in the car with S, wanted to choose whether or not to eat the squirrel at the end of day, or of the world.

The truth was, too, that despite his wholehearted protest, Pablo sensed some validity in the binary—loyalty, autonomy—but he also sensed that, like most things he cared about, whatever validity it had was suspect. Desire is a moving target—that's really all he meant to communicate in his conversations about exclusivity with Z—and the kinds of social desire that translate to apparent loyalty could easily get confused for the kinds that translate to apparent autonomy. Just watch people trying to decide which way to go mid-protest, into the kettle or back to safety.

Or back to obligation, safe or not.

Just watch a person like that, he thought. Or be one.

Pablo was getting muddled. He was only half paying attention to these thoughts, because he was also half paying attention to the scene in the tent. Marina had stepped out as soon as he entered—she didn't say why, or where she was going—and he was sitting at the table feeling invisible, literally as if the other vendors (Is that what they were? Was he *vending* "communication"?) could not apperceive his existence. He was muddled, but he knew at least that he didn't want to be thinking about arrests at protests right now; the last time had left a bad taste in his mouth. In a sense, it's what drove him east to the village (Pablo was not from the city to the south but from a different, more distant city to the west). And going east to the village was how he'd met Z.

He took out his notebook, recalling that he'd promised to record the day's events. But how do you record events you don't, you can't, understand? There was a din in the tent, but it didn't sound like language. There was a louder din in his head, which also didn't sound like language, but the din in his head was impossible to ignore. It was like that scene behind his eyelids earlier, the flood of deep fuchsia with the bright magenta spot in its center: a scene of conflictual actions (let it in, keep it out).

It was as loud, in that way, as the sun.

Pablo wrote in his notebook: "Who was it who believed that all language was a translation of an urtext that nobody can read?"

He skipped a line and wrote: "Whose term is 'detranslation'?"

He skipped another line and wrote: "I am ashamed at my lack of memory; I should know much more than I do."

And then: "If I don't find a way to make myself useful here, I will explode."

By the time Marina found her way back to the table, Pablo had come to some conclusions.

"I think we are participating in a shared hallucination," he said by way of greeting, and handed Marina another cookie.

"I think what has happened is that the doubts we each have about the validity of what we do—the validity of the Zeno's paradox that describes our work toward shared meaning, shared understanding, the rejection of borders, attempted agreement of any sort, all under the conditions of imperfection that are inherent in these pursuits—those doubts have, for the moment, won."

"I'm listening," Marina responded, unblinking eyes.

"I think this tent is our field of inquiry, made half real. That it's the urtext for our running inner monologues, in a sense."

Pablo seemed pleased with his interpretation, which did not come out quite as fully formed as it's quoted here but still showed signs of a hyper-assuredness that made Marina, two decades his elder, restrain an impulse to be annoyed.

"Do you mean," she began while also reality testing Pablo's theory by trying to make eye contact with one after another of the people behind the white plastic tables, "that our services—Division of Conflict, Division of Conversation—aren't really needed here?" Her mouth completed her question as her eyes completed their sweep of the tent; none of its other occupants' gazes, even those that appeared to be directed her way, registered acknowledgment.

"I mean," Pablo responded after a pause, "that before we are able to be of use, we are here to adjust something about our expectations. Or maybe about more than our expectations."

"Adjust what, exactly?" Marina asked. She could feel a sense of resistance or defensiveness grip her abdomen. She had spent her career questioning and recalibrating the assumptions of her field. She knew from adjusting expectations.

"I don't know." Pablo hung his head, or assumed the aura of a person hanging their head. Marina forgave him immediately for his self-congratulatory tone before.

"Nor I," she said. "But given that nobody seems to be able to see or hear us, I'm inclined to agree with you that something weird is going on."

COFFEE

While S and E were driving to the meeting, the others gradually assembled at the café-bar at which E still worked part-time, ostensibly, most businesses in the village having provisionally shut down because of the water situation, or just because owners and staff had been occupied elsewhere, otherwise.

The café-bar's owner had been away on vacation when Ezekiel hit and had not been in touch since, and the second worker at the café-bar was stranded at home, cut off with eight or nine other houses tucked behind the collapsed bridge on Old County Route 12. E had given Leslie and Kim the code to the emergency lockbox, correctly assuming that of the Anti-Love group (herself included), one of them would be the most likely to arrive early and the most capable of double boiling a kettle of water and making coffee in one of the café-bar's large-capacity, insulated French presses.

As it happens, they had arrived at the same time, in a carpool, since they lived not far apart, and figured the coffee out together, so that now, while E and S became the last ones to show up, the rest—five members of Anti-Love and four newcomers from Love—mingled awkwardly as they waited for it to brew.

An outsider would have thought it was an AA meeting or the first session of a therapy group. An outsider would have sensed that before long these strangers would be revealing more than an ordinary portion of themselves to one another.

FIGURE EIGHTEEN

Pablo saw it first. He covered his eyes with both palms, resisting the impulse to rub them, cartoon-style, instead waiting a few breaths and then pulling his hands away.

"What is it?" asked Marina. She was flipping pages in the Manual, agitated. "I know, it's weird. It's like nobody sees us."

Pablo pointed.

"Oh. Yeah, and those things are getting realer."

That Pablo knew what she meant by this didn't surprise Marina any more than it surprised Pablo that Marina seemed to be seeing what he saw.

"How many do you see?"

"I count ten."

"Me too. Do you think . . ."

"One for each table?"

"They don't seem to be indexed to particular tables."

"How do we know if they aren't?"

"And there are eleven tables, anyway. Twelve, counting us."

"That one's empty. Its person never showed up."

They fell silent. One of the ten figures became realer than the others—to use Marina's term, which is as good as any—while the others reverted.

"What would you call that?" asked Pablo, unconsciously beginning to sketch the thing on a blank page of his notebook.

"I'd call it a tower," Marina said, cocking her head to the left as she considered what she was looking at. "Or a pillar, or pedestal. But a hollow one."

She laughed. "I don't mean that to sound so symbolic! I just mean it's taller than it is fat, and it just doesn't seem . . . solid, somehow. Fragile—or *fallible,* that's the word that comes to mind. Though I can't see any visual evidence for whether or not I'm right."

Pablo laughed too, a single wry huff.

For a minute, Marina continued to look at the tower or pillar or pedestal, trying to force herself to imagine it as a solid thing, while Pablo scratched away in his notebook.

"Here," he said, sliding the book over to Marina. "This is how that figure appears to me."

WAITING

You may have noticed how much time people are spending waiting for something to occur, or waiting, perhaps, for something to be revealed. When E was narrating, she apologized for not telling a story in a satisfying way. But of course, the story of waiting is as old as the sun. So no apologies here.

You may yourself be waiting, for instance, for news from other quarters, parts of E's world that have apparently fallen away: from the bookstore clerk (or from both bookstore clerks, the one with the cherry lips and the one with the forgettable name but the memorable hands); from the husband and the wife or the wayward daughter, or any of the mentor's (now we can say Marina's) clients whose numbers remain undialed in E's phone. You may be wondering what happened to Giorgos the Greek, or what became, finally, of the capitalist. You may be wondering whether you've seen the end of the News Reports.

You may be waiting for E to be handed back the narration.

You may be waiting for something else.

If you resist or even resent being told what you may be waiting for, you aren't original, which is another way of saying you aren't alone.

If you enjoy it, you have company too. We switch back and forth, most of us, between awaiting and providing stories, something graspable to give us hope.

We switch back and forth with each other, the analyst would remind us, but also with ourselves.

Forget hope. For something graspable at all.

⁊

At the table where the migrated members of Love and the current members of Anti-Love (or however it may refer to itself now) had gathered, people sat with their mugs of coffee and took up E's invitation to introduce themselves. It was orderly; everyone took their turn. Something about the circumstance—the emergency that wasn't, or that was not yet a *personal* emergency for any of the gathered—something about the abstract thinking that had led to the concrete decision to gather, brought a calm to the room, a collective low blood pressure that translated into something like a collective restraint.

Of course there would be an exception to this. There is always an exception to a provisional state of calm.

QUESTIONS TO LEARN MORE ABOUT UNDERLYING ISSUES

Marina stared at the page in Pablo's notebook. The figure he had drawn had nothing to do with what she had seen across the tent; this didn't surprise her, or rather it surprised her without surprising her, in that way that surprise can become, temporarily or open-endedly, the norm—not "the new normal," a phrase Marina hated unequivocally, but just a matter of course, the way watching a person move from one stage of life to another seemingly all at once, as a child moves into adolescence or a parent into old age, can feel both real and surreal at the same time. At least for a person whose age falls squarely between the two.

Or the way, she imagined, a military coup might feel, though she had never experienced a military coup. Marina was a mediator but not on the level of governments, of nations. She hated nations. And to be honest, she didn't love the people she knew professionally who worked with them. She was a mediator on the level of pairs, of family units of all kinds, collaborators, and small groups. She had worked with a theater troupe and with a bicycle-repair collective. She had worked with countless court-assigned teens and their guardians. Her bread and butter, or maybe just the butter: bourgeois divorces, of which she needed to take on only two or three a year to effectively subsidize the rest of her work.

She didn't know why she was thinking of a military coup now. It had nothing to do with the figure Pablo had drawn in his notebook, though it was true that the object he'd sketched seemed somehow more threatening than the pillar or tower or pedestal she herself had seen.

"What's the worst collective trauma you've lived through?" she found herself saying out loud, both to Pablo and not to Pablo. She said it into the room.

Even as she spoke, she was correcting her previous thought. She could not imagine, really, how a military coup (setting aside the sense in which, structurally, she might have known nothing else her whole life) might feel, only how it would feel to read the news that such a thing was happening where she lived, closer to home than usual. She could not really imagine tanks on the street outside her door, only images of tanks on the street outside the doors of people she knew. She could only imagine a thing like that coming *closer*. She didn't know how to imagine it coming *all the way*, breaching her sense of the permanence of the inevitable, dull status quo. Her conversations—the pricklier, less fluid ones—with E had often circled around this, she now realized, but she had never quite understood. What drew E to mediation was different from what had drawn Marina to it so long ago. What E appreciated about Marina's evolving revision of classic techniques was, yes, the emphasis on seeking from each party the story beneath the story. But there was also a distinction to be made between their senses of what a story was.

There is a way in which the points of resistance between Marina and E mirror those that occur, not often but consistently, between E and S, the ones that were first revealed when E described something about the experience of being repeatedly stabbed while reading, and S wondered aloud (which is to say in a message, at the time) at the necessity of repeatedly submitting oneself to such a thing.

❦

Pablo was saying, ". . . a story I heard separately from each of my older relatives, about their houses being stormed and occupied, about inflation and rationing and famine and sudden deaths, and I could never make it add up to something coherent. But growing up with so much of my extended family near me, you could say I lived through it in a secondary way. I know people study this exact phenomenon, but I haven't. I haven't been interested in giving it a name."

The tent door opened, letting in the brightest light so far, then closed, and a small figure entered, turned, and walked into a dark corner. Soon the air was so full of music Pablo could not have kept talking, or Marina could not have kept listening. The sound was of a rising, swirling piano improvisation in a complex minor key; Pablo thought automatically of Abdullah Ibrahim (fka "Dollar Brand"), and Marina thought automatically of Emahoy Tsegué-Maryam Guèbrou (aka "the nun"), and in fact the playing was like a conversation between the two musicians, the way it moved swiftly between intensity and calm, ground and sky.

Too binary, Pablo thought aloud to Marina's suggestion, which had also been thought aloud. Ground and sky is wrong.

The swirling piano built further in decibels and complexity, a cascade without regard for gravity. A swarm, or a battalion. As it passed a certain volume, it ceased to be identifiable as piano music; low hums emerged from below that might have been digital drones or low-throated singing; upper registers dropped in from above, pulsing: insect communication patterns or the last frantic rise of an EDM song as the higher frequencies, filtered out until close to the end, are let through.

As the music turned dance, the tent turned club, the sunlight turned away as artificial blue and yellow and red patterns illuminated the white canvas walls, bouncing their low saturated light off the rippled plastic windows. The people turned dance club, too, vendors climbing over and around their tables and into the center of the space, a continuous stream of new bodies now entering through the door and joining together on the floor. Pablo and Marina watched as the population doubled, then tripled, as the bodies shook and spun and found and lost each other across the unheeded painted boundaries (basketball, dodgeball); they watched shoulders and backs and asses and hands engage and disengage, each body unique but all of them together; and none of it was strange or unfamiliar to the translator and the mediator still seated behind their shared table, they had each had their moments, many and frequent, on floors like this, but all of it was a surprise in *this* moment, all of it faster and more unmoored, and so much *louder*, both aurally and visually, than anything either one could specifically remember. They watched as a body was passed around the room atop hands atop other bodies that continued to dance beneath the weight; they watched as a body in a wheelchair spun at the center of a group, countless hands contributing in unison to the spin; they watched as a group on one side of the tent took its moves to the floor and a group on the other side took its to the air; they watched until they began to sense, first one of them and then the other, that this was not a show that would end, that this was no interlude and there was no mass exhaustion in sight, and when they sensed this they also sensed the appetite to join, and they crawled over their plastic table and separated into the crowd.

FIGURE NINETEEN

This one looks like a parasite. Which is to say that it takes the shape of what a person believes—right or wrong—to be unfortunate but necessary, and attaches like a puzzle piece to the person's most vulnerable, porous part. Unable to feed itself, it takes its fuel from the intensity of this kind of individual belief, rerouting the train of energy and commitment to its chosen destination.

For example:

A person feels guilt, or sorrow, and wishes to transform the feeling into something outside the boundaries of self. The parasite takes this desire for transformation and offers a false path—energetic self-loathing, most often, or immobilizing self-doubt—which provides a false sense of escape while keeping the energy inside the system. A system to which the parasite now belongs.

Figure nineteen is dangerous not only to individuals but also, more dramatically, to the group. Its story is a version of gaslighting. Its defense, what makes it so resistant to being found out and killed, is a version of the Drunkard's Search.

The tent party showed no sign of letting up, but it did show signs of eventually burning out; how long could people continue to swarm and agitate at this pace? The sensory stimulation was at peak or beyond, the capacity of the tent at peak or beyond, Marina danced with her eyes open and began seeing things, and the things she was seeing made her think of DMT, with which she was familiar from her studies but not from personal experience. Pablo danced with his eyes closed and began seeing things, and what he saw also made him think of DMT, with which he had personal experience but the study of which, as with those phenomena called *epigenetics* and *intergenerational trauma,* he had chosen to avoid.

There was no perceptible break, no segue between this scene and the scene that followed, which was in some sense just a return to the previous scene.

Pablo and Marina sat at their table, Marina flipping through her Manual and Pablo taking out his tobacco pouch and removing a pinch from his dwindling supply. Each of the eleven other tables—save one—was tended by a vendor, but now, as Pablo and Marina would discover once they lifted their focus from their tasks, those vendors were able to notice their presence. A child in a dress sat at a spinet piano in a dark corner of the tent, practicing scales.

Once they lifted their focus from their tasks, Marina and Pablo would also notice that the takers for each vendor's service were carrying items, blenders and televisions and sewing machines, cracked pitchers and broken chairs, sometimes waiting in lines or in groupings of three or four around a particular station, sometimes quietly solitary and sometimes chatting vigorously with their neighbors. But instead of lifting their focus and seeing all of this, Marina continued to reread the chapter called "Setting the Tone," and Pablo made a beeline for the door.

The person who approached Marina's table was wearing an orange vest over coveralls and mud-splattered muck boots and held a walkie-talkie, a spiral notebook, and a pen. Marina listened to the person for a minute, then took a minute to gather her things, and in another minute, she was following the person who'd come to fetch her across the floor and outside.

Pablo dropped the dead end of his smoke to the ground and reentered the tent, barely noting that the door sign now read simply REPAIR CAFÉ. At the top of the sign was typed the name of what elsewhere we have called the neighboring town.

TWO GROUPS INTRODUCING THEMSELVES

Marc:

"O.K., I guess I'll start. I'm Marc, I'm—oh, he/him/his—I'm in advertising. I mean, I'm a poet, but I work—I've been working—in advertising. Freelance. Women's cosmetics. [Pause.] I never lead with what I do for money, not sure why I just did. Weird. I'm a—I guess I organize. I work with empty-lot reclamation in the city. I mean, not for pay. I make the posters, social media, outreach materials . . . anyway. So I wasn't sure if I'd come up, but then I did—I mean, I'm here for a bit. I'm, uh, trained in Swedish massage, weirdly. So, you know, if you're stressed. Ha. I guess I'm—I don't know. Can I stop there?"

Leslie:

"I'm Leslie—she/her, for now—hi, everyone, and welcome. So, I don't know, by way of introduction. Hmm. Well, I keep thinking about—I wonder if any of you have heard of this thing, I'm kind of obsessed—the Rose of Leary? Here, I'll draw it. [Leslie draws on a whiteboard that has been leaned up against the wall.] O.K., so it's not a personality test, per se, but more of a tool for decoding dynamics when they happen, and for intentionally modifying your behavior to rebalance things that have gone off. So it's not that one of us is an Above person and one a Below person—or one an Opposed and one a Together—but that when you—like, if Kim or whoever were to interrupt me right now he'd be displaying Above behavior, and if he were interrupting me because he was worried about time, afraid that we'd run out of time before everyone could be introduced, or whatever, I mean, we have nothing but time at the moment so that's a bad example, but anyway, if that was why he interrupted then he would actually be displaying Above-Together behavior, which is basically dominant but supposedly beneficent, and I'd likely respond by agreeing with him and cutting myself off, which would basically be the submissive position, but all in the interest of togetherness, so the point is that if Kim were to interrupt me but in an aggressive way—sorry Kim, I'm just using you as an example!—to, like, insult me or just to take over the conversation, then I'd have a different response, still submissive but also either rebellious or withdrawn. See how it maps onto this wheel?

[Pause; Leslie takes a breath.]

"So yeah, I just am always drawn to these oversimplifications, I guess because I wonder if there's something to them.

"The 'Leary' is actually Tim Leary, before the acid days—I can't remember if I said that already. Anyway, one of the ideas associated with this theory is that Together behavior triggers Together behavior. And after I learned about this, for a while I was constantly trying to test that theory in practice. I think it held more often than not. But yeah, too schematic, right? I dunno. Sorry, that was a weird introduction. Um, I'm a Libra and I'm allergic to shellfish?"

E BRIEFLY COMMANDEERS THE NARRATIVE

I'm sorry for interrupting the introductions when they've hardly begun, but I'm worried this is heading down a path that will lead us to ruin. Dramatic, I know. Sorry.

Do you remember when I said, "Don't be fooled by the present tense, the future tense, when they occur?" When I said, "This is a story about the past, it's already over"?

Perhaps this—the story, its present form—is leading us not to ruin, but to ruins: to the past, or the historical past, at least. To the history of love and loss, the history of love's foreclosing definition at the hands of commerce and adaptive cynicism, of the state and of vocabulary (marriage, romance, possession), which is to say the history of literature, philosophy, politics, theory, post-theory . . . Isn't that exactly what we're trying to avoid? Are we all just going to sit around the table, talking about ideas? Putting ideas about love—Love—on a pillar or a pedestal, then taking turns knocking them down? Or is that what it means—all it means—to interpret the world while also living in it?

I'm embarrassed by what I'm saying, yes. But I'm not sure I trust that this new narrator, without anything clear at stake, could have a sense of the frame. Isn't embarrassment, which requires both humility and self-consciousness, the most powerful focusing device? Flawed, but at least it can be tracked. I'm thinking about Giorgos the Greek, his bald attempt to parse desire, his obvious internal references to characters (people, real ones) I would never know, even by description or name.

I'm thinking of the song my friends' band, years ago, would play a version of to close each show, a dumb and delirious collision between Sappho "38" ("you burn me") and Mellencamp '82 ("hurts so good").

I'm thinking, scrolling back just months (Or only weeks? I forget), of the capitalist's nipples—of the name, if one exists, for the feeling he would have experienced in the precise moment when he grabbed my arm and froze me in the pull.

You'll protest that that was *my* fantasy, that the capitalist might have no taste for the scald. That he might just have been caught off guard, and stopped things as soon as he noticed he was able to. That he might want, and might *want* to want, only the falsely advertised modern prize— comfort and titillation in the same package, each on demand—and thus be doomed. But you'd be wrong, or rather your argument would be flawed, though you might be right about the capitalist.

For one thing: that the prize is falsely advertised does not mean (a) that the picture of it is complete or (b) that it is impossible. Every writer lives things that can't be written.

After what's happened recently with S, you might ask me: E, are you in Love? And I can only say, if I'm being truthful—and why not?—that I'm afraid I am. Which is to say that I am in love, and that I am afraid.

But that isn't how I'll introduce myself to this group when my turn comes, after Marc and Leslie and Kim and Stella and R and R and S and the rest take theirs, and after I've stepped away and taken my place among the others, arrayed around a table sipping boiled-and-cooled water (and, yes, facing S in public for the first time).

I really am sorry for the interruption. It rose up in me at once and nonnegotiably. Like a bout of hiccups or a sneeze. And now it's done.

along the lines already established by Marc and Leslie: Kim teased Leslie about casting him in her example, dissipating the real tension that casting had caused; R (from Love, who introduced herself as Rinda) spoke eloquently about her ambivalence, as a person who had been raised in a village much like this one and fled it for the city decades ago, at finding herself in the role of interloping "flatlander"; another R (also from Love) made everybody laugh with a self-deprecating introduction that hid real anxiety about losing access to their familiar hookup sources (this routine included a spontaneous live demo of one of their favorite apps, which disproved, in real time, any worries that the regional scene wouldn't be able to provide them); Stella (from Anti-Love, the one who was quiet through both versions of *Gaslight*) didn't say much, because she never said much, but what she did say—"I'm kinda freaked out, honestly. And confused."—before stopping and staring into a point in the distance with a small tight smile on her lips, created an opening.

The opening was filled, this time, by an exchange between Leslie and S, in which S called bullshit on the Rose of Leary, rising from the table to pick up a marker and declare an intention to "edit" the diagram, then putting down the pen, picking up the whiteboard and standing it on its head. "That's a cheap trick," Leslie said, and S said, "I know, but what can it tell us?" and everyone stared at the upside-down whiteboard, now with "Under" (upside down) at the top and "Above" (upside down) at the bottom, and each of the people around the table tilted their head to the left or to the right the way you do when trying to read upside down, until some-body—it was Stella, though it could have been anyone—tilted too far and fell off her chair, and finally everyone was able to laugh a non-nervous laugh.

When the doorbell jingled as Margaret walked in, 5:00 on the nose, unfazed by the increased occupancy in the café-bar as compared to what she found on her usual rounds, and walked around the table offering her braided leather cuffs—some natural brown and some black and some an unexpected safety orange—each present member of Love and each present member of Anti-Love wanted one, and some who didn't have cash were covered by others who did, and Margaret ignored their polite questions unless they directly related to the goods, and sold out of her supply just before reaching E (who was last in the circuit and already wore two of the things), and then she frowned and appended a "Sorry!" to her customary "o.k., thank you, bye!" And then Margaret crossed the room, hoisting her bag higher on her shoulder, and pushed out onto the street.

WHAT IS AND ISN'T PREDICTABLE

The predictability of Margaret's incursion into the café-bar—a predictability recognized by E and communicated to the table after Margaret had left and as the members of the groups (now one group, as far as a stranger, or Margaret, for that matter, could tell) fastened the bracelets around one another's wrists—was not, it would turn out, going to be the exception. The new group formed by the dregs of the two groups was feeling, collectively, a wave of disorientation. In the conversation that followed Margaret's interruption, this collective wave of disorientation was individualized— people sharing details of the situations they had left, roommates, bills, in one case a violent partner, in one case a brutalizing boss; but also people sharing information and predictions based on the "near miss" the media had declared following the storm's pass over the city, and the earthquakes that followed, devastating to some quarters but not injuring enough to those in charge for the massive changes everyone in this room agreed were necessary to imminently result.

All of this was, of course, predictable: the near miss and the full hit being experienced at the same time, but by different people; the disappearance of the café-bar's owner and second worker; the appearance of Margaret on cue. There is very little that is not, as Leslie pointed out, predictable. There are other outcomes that would have been equally so: the full-blown Armageddon suggested earlier (the disaster-novel plot); a smaller, more intimate apocalypse of cruelty between these particular few; or any number of ways the circumstances could have conformed to a different dice roll. But what happened was both a lot and not very much. Somehow, each person around the table (not everyone was still around the table; some had risen to explore the café-bar and inspect the contents of the fridge, others had gone out front to smoke) had wound up here.

A philosopher of Choice whom E had learned of from Marina held the view that "difficult" choices are made not by deciding which path is right, but by deciding—by intuiting—which choice the chooser is able, at the moment in question, to commit to.

This was a room of people who had committed to being in this room.

BELOW

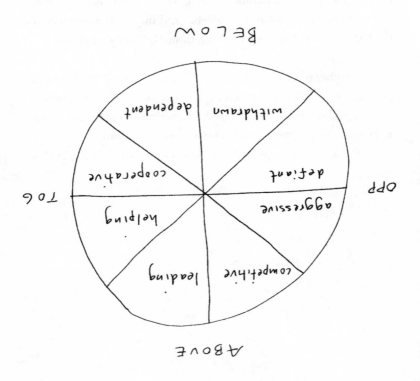

OPP

withdrawn | dependent

defiant | cooperative

aggressive | helping

TOG

competitive | leading

ABOVE

180

PABLO SENDS A POSTCARD

It's lucky he has only a postcard's worth of sentences to communicate to Z, he thinks.

He was thinking about her on the bus ride, and he was thinking about her as he smoked outside, between exiting the tent and reentering it, only half noting the typed sign's third and final transformation.

He was thinking about her, or rather about that parting conversation with her, as he smoked and as he watched a pair of crows chase each other through a cluster of leafless trees. Loyalty, autonomy, loyalty, autonomy. He felt like the most loyal person on earth; it had hurt to hear Z suggest that wasn't true. Now he laughed. Who but a sociopath or a utilitarian would self-define as not loyal?

A person who doesn't like laws, he thought. And a person for whom the etymologies of words are, for better or for worse, always announcing themselves, for whom a word's origin is worn on its sleeve. Loyal. Legal. Royal. Regal.

So, an anarchist. So, a translator. An anarchist translator may be the least loyal non-sociopathic person in the world, he thought. (Leaving aside actual utilitarians, and Pablo never knew quite what to make of them.)

He pulled the fuzzy-edged postcard out from his notebook, where he was using it as a bookmark. It had on the front of it the picture of a waterfall foregrounded by a grouping of sightseers seen from the back, with a pair of gleaming 1950's cars in a parking lot at the edge. He couldn't remember when or where he'd picked it up.

The back was age stained but free of handwriting. Pablo wrote on it without thinking first about what he'd write:

"Brutal honesty is usually more brutal than it is honest," he wrote in big block letters on half of the postcard, to the left of the vertical dividing line. He wrote Z's name to the right side of the line and then remembered that she hadn't gone to her sister's as she'd first planned, that she'd changed course at the last minute and gone to a place he had no address for—friends outside Austin, a camper van in a yard—and the whole point of writing a postcard was to contact her unidirectionally, requiring no reply. He didn't want to text, or email, or call. Anyway, it could wait. He crossed out Z's name and instead translated his sentence, filling the right half of the card.

A person in coveralls with an orange vest, carrying a clipboard and a pencil, approached.

As he walked away from the tent on the heels of the orange-vested person, Pablo deposited his bilingual postcard-sign into the crotch of two branches in the nearest tree.

MARINA TAKES A BREAK

She was not expecting to be sitting in a small wall tent—a miniature version of the original tent in which she had met Pablo—for
three hours, behind a wooden desk, doing what could be described
as the speed dating of mediation work. This tent was more fur-
nished, less provisional feeling than the large one: in addition to
the wooden table and the chair she sat in, there were three other
wooden chairs; a red-and-beige braided wool rug on the floor,
smelling slightly musty; a few lanterns (solar, she guessed, based on
the wires that led, through a hole above one of the windows, to the
outside) hanging from the metal tent frame; an old putty-colored
metal file cabinet with a key lock; and a potted fern. "It's the therapy room. Also Reiki, that kind of thing, in regular times," the
person in the orange vest had said while ushering Marina through
the unwindowed flap door. It made Marina think of nothing more
than a game her niece had shown her the last time they'd been
able to have a visit—Animal Crossroads or Animal Tracking, she
couldn't remember exactly—in which tents like this, each deco-
rated for a particular use, were inhabited by wise cartoon owls or
industrious cartoon squirrels, ready to provide services to the play-
er's avatar, about which all she could remember was a rear view of a
small cartoon figure wearing a wide-brimmed hat.

Since sitting down, she had talked to four pairs of neighbors trying to work out cost shares for various damages to shared prop-
erty (driveways, mostly, and in one case a revenue-bringing apple
orchard that was affected unequally across the two neighbors'

lands); she had talked to three employee-employer pairs arguing about the terms of furloughs, layoffs, and forced temporary leaves. (Her method required her to speak first and longest to the employees; one had come alone, to seek advice about negotiating with his parents, who were also his employers—this was, coincidentally, the brother of Stella from Anti-Love.) She had talked to two separating or recently separated couples who wound up sharing quarters because one of their homes had been flooded beyond repair. One pair was doing fine but wanted, proactively, to seek a more formal agreement about their situation. The other was a nightmare of intractable brutality, the kind of case that left Marina numb— her only defense against the alternative, a sense of impotence accompanied by a crushing shame at the stated goals of her chosen profession—and prompted her to put a "Back in Ten" sign on the door and to leave her "office" for a walk.

The forest was thick with slender trees, something she hadn't noticed until now. "All of these trees are the same age," she thought, though she was hopeless at identifying the different species: ash, birch, aspen, beech, every tree name a short word beginning with *a* or *b*, all of them registering to Marina only as *tree*. Among them were a few pines, which she was able to identify at least as *evergreen*. Wandering among them, she came upon a single, much larger tree, with giant jagged leaves already beginning to turn red. Maple, she thought, embarrassed to feel an attendant infusion of pride.

One of the branches of the giant maple—its trunk was wider than Marina's shoulders—had fallen in the storm and created a kind of slanted bench. Marina sat and reached into her jacket pocket out of habit, as if she'd find a pack of cigarettes there. Instead she found a folded-up note. When had she last worn this jacket? She couldn't recall.

The note was in her own handwriting, apparently taken during or just after a conversation she must have wanted to remember. It said:

What is a person besides Capacity + Temperament +
Experience? And which one is on top? Studies re: rock / paper
/ scissors = amateurs tend to pick rock. Associations of strength,
etc. Strategy is to pick paper when playing with amateur.
Which of capacity / temperament / experience is paper?

She returned to an empty tent, its dusk-activated solar lights now dimly aglow. No more takers, for now.

THE NEWS REPORTS

The news is terrible. You have to read between the lines. You have to let the margins challenge you (you have to like to be challenged). What if the desire to be challenged could be taught, could be learned? Is this the syllabus E is seeking, and others too? A top who knows how much pain to dole out per thrill, how much thrill per unit of pain? Or a relation fit to withstand an occasional, painful misstep?

They tried combining their syllabi, and then they tried rewriting them, and then they threw all the drafts in a pile. When they gathered, they asked for help and they let off steam, and sometimes they read aloud. They moved in with each other and swapped spots until it worked. At some point Kim disclosed that he didn't like to sit, and now at meetings he wanders the room, occasionally jolting into a little sprint. They found out Kim had been named after Stan Robinson, the utopian novelist and an old family friend. They learned that MN had been raised on the road. Stella started taking notes and passing them around; the first read "I have a hard time talking in front of more than four of five people." (They found out Stella had been allowed, at four, to name herself.)

Their agendas, if they were recorded, would be embarrassing, constituted by questions. (1) How do we keep the edges of our or any groups porous while still retaining enough history to not start at zero with each meeting? (2) How can we use imagination to pry fear from oppression? (2a) (How) can we protect each other during bouts of acute fear, individual or shared? (2b) What is the difference between transformative, shared fear and diffuse or performative empathy? (2c) If it isn't possible to feel another person's fear, what is possible in its stead?

They asked these questions in meetings but also outside of them. Each had individual questions that merged like cars on a highway; sometimes one or more of them went off on their own, or they left in groups of twos or threes or fours. Some of them put their arms around each other, some fucked. One might be accidentally pregnant and is living through the wait-and-see.

They did all of this in the context of the village, which itself was changing, both quickly and at a crawl; it turned out, E found, that the village wasn't as underpopulated as she had believed, that there were just a lot of people who didn't come to Main Street, who hadn't wanted or needed to come into the café-bar or even to walk by its windows. Some of those people now came in while the two groups—formerly two groups, now one—met. The lights were still on (thanks to autopay, they assumed), and E's pay kept showing up in her account too, though she didn't know how long that would last. One day the second worker—Iana—walked in and joined the rest as if she'd been there from the start. Iana brought her own syllabus and added it to the pile; it came from the perspective of liberation theology, and expanded the group's discussions in ways they did not expect.

Margaret came in daily, was now making other things from her leather: leashes, belts, wallets. Everyone bought a wallet, though they hardly used them anymore. The next time Margaret came in, she asked for a coffee and drank it quietly at the counter before shuffling off.

Most of these changes had to do with the collapse of the main bridge, which hadn't happened right away but only after enough time had passed for the washed-out ground beneath it to fail. It wasn't a permanent or complete isolation, but it didn't have a known end. People settled in.

A game of musical chairs had deposited them here, where they were: in the village, or in the case of Pablo and Marina, in the neighboring town, and each knew how lucky they were to have gotten a chair at all. They were haunted both collectively and individually by the knowledge that despite their ability to adjust, their surprising ability to appreciate the chairs in which they'd landed, there is always one fewer chair than is needed. One person without a chair. That was what they knew, a fact as incontrovertible as time, as gravity.

But even gravity, or the conceptualization of gravity, had to be taught. Let alone the concept, or the conceptualization of time.

If the concept of the missing chair had appeared explicitly on the syllabus of their childhoods instead of being transmitted by way of a game, if it had been presented as a fact that could provoke instinctual dissent, things might have been different. Mightn't they have? Not just for them, but for everyone?

LOSSES

The clerk, the other clerk, the capitalist, the husband and the wife, the runaway teen and her dad. The ideas of Love and of Anti-Love. Many people's jobs. The Argentine analyst. The vendor from the eleventh table, and that vendor's unknown sign.

The anarchist of Science, or anti-Science.

Z, of course.

Figures twenty through twenty-seven, but who's counting?

The question of which losses are permanent is open, as is that of which ones are desired. The sky at night is open. The bodega is open, almost all the time. The books are open, too, even the ones that have been forgotten, willfully or not. Even those obscured by a blur.

I would like to count embarrassment as a loss—the undue kind, at least. E and I share that wish with each other, and we offer it to you.

AUTOECIOUS END-STOPPED TANKA

E and S sat in the living room on pillows, backs against the wall. Stella had moved into the second bedroom; her mom had kicked her out for refusing to pay rent. E's laptop was open to the dictionary. The earliest known appearance of "musical chairs" is from 1877, *Merriam-Webster* says; no further citation is provided.

Other terms added in 1877 include:

autoecious

autogamy

belly button

bookie

Camembert

check valve

deathwatch beetle

Decembrist

end-stopped

erotomania

field guide

fruit bat

gang hook

gegenschein

hoopla

hornswoggle

ingot iron

in re

jokester

jungle cat
kulak
limbus
macromere
nerve cord
ontological argument
primary root
rain tree
safety net
tanka
turnbuckle
underfur
vespid
work camp
xenophobia
yantra
and zymogen

They sat cross-legged on the floor looking up definitions. Behind
the closed door, Stella was singing, or warming up to sing: unbro-
ken arced scales moving from chest voice to head voice and back
again. E and S looked at each other; nobody knew Stella sang.

They agreed Stella's voice was beautiful. They agreed it was time
for a drink. They laughed about how agreeable they were, but not
without voicing their fear it would end. They agreed they should
close the screen, but not before agreeing on the best word from the
list. *Gegenschein*: a faint light about twenty degrees across on the
celestial sphere opposite the sun
    probably caused by
    backscatter of sunlight by
    solar-system dust.

ACKNOWLEDGMENTS

Thank you: Adrian Shirk, Akin Akinwumi, Amanda Annis, Ann Holder, Anne Elizabeth Moore, Barbara Browning, Bushel Collective, BC Revolutionary Feminisms Reading Group, BC Writers Group, Carla Valadez, Christopher Grau, Claire Donato, Communist Research Cluster, Daley Farr, Dana Spiotta, David Naimon, Deepika Marya and Leah Wing, Ellie Ga, Erika Stevens, Gordon Dahlquist, Iris Cushing, Jared Fagen, Jennifer Kabat, Jonathan Lethem, Kellie M. Hultgren, Laura Taylor, Laura Wood, Lewis Freedman, Lisa Anne Auerbach, Lizzie Davis, Lyric Hunter, Marco Breuer, Marit Swanson, Mina Takahashi, Mirene Arsanios, Pareesa Pourian, Renee Gladman, Roz Foster, Simone White, and volunteers on the *Watershed Post* liveblog (2011); the staff at Coffee House Press; Headlands Center for the Arts; my family and my friends. This is a work of fiction. Some of the places and situations are based, to some degree, on places that exist and events that have occurred. The characters populating these places and situations are made up.

Thanks to all the publications referenced within these pages, and to those who wrote, translated, edited, published, and let me know about them. The quotes on p.16 are from *Three Dialogues on Knowledge* by Paul Feyerabend (Wiley-Blackwell, 1991). The quote on pp. 21–22 is from "Intuitionism in the Philosophy of Mathematics" by Rosalie Imhoff (*Stanford Encyclopedia of Philosophy*, fall 2020 edition). The book on p. 33 is *The Guérillères* by Monique Wittig, translated by David Le Vay (Picador, 1972). The book on p. 35 is *Intimacy* by Jean-Paul Sartre, translated by Lloyd Alexander (Avon, 1938). The book on p. 39 is *A Dialogue on Love* by Eve Kosofsky Sedgwick (Beacon Press, 1999). The book on p. 45 is *G* by John Berger (Weidenfeld & Nicolson, 1972). The book on p. 54 is *Restaurant Samsara* by Daniel Owen (Furniture Press, 2018). The quote on p. 62 is from the essay "Freedom" by D. W. Winnicott. The book on p. 69 is *Living a Feminist Life* by Sara Ahmed, narrated by Larissa Gallagher (Duke University Press, 2017). The book on pp. 75–76 is *Signs Preceding the End of the World* by Yuri Herrera, translated by Lisa Dillman (And Other Stories, 2015). The language on pp. 94–96 and 98 is adapted from the archive of the 24/7 liveblog hosted and run by the *Watershed Post* and staffed in part by community volunteers, including myself, to provide information to residents of Delaware County, NY, and surrounding counties affected by Tropical Cyclone Irene in August 2011. The book on pp. 102–103 is *The Glass Bead Game (Magister Ludi)* by Herman Hesse, translated by Richard and Clara Winston (Holt, Rinehart & Winston, 1943). The book on p. 117 is *The Desert* by Brandon Shimoda (The Song Cave, 2018). The language in "Aspects of Questioning" on p. 150 is taken from "Mediation Manual" (© Mediation Manual 1999 revised edition, Wing; Mediation Manual © 1991 Wing and Marden-Cruz) and used by permission. Though this language and some ideas about mediation were directly inspired by a 2016 training in mediation with a social justice perspective led by Deepika Marya and Leah Wing, interpretations of that material are my own and don't necessarily reflect the specifics of Marya and Wing's training. The artist's book on p. 153 is *As you sow so you reap* by Lisa Anne Auerbach (Private risograph edition, 2022). An earlier version of the opening of this book was published under the title "Love, Anti- (notes toward)" online at *Black Sun Lit* (April 11, 2018). Thanks to Jared Daniel Fagen. The text from the "postcards" on pp. 93, 97, and 99 is taken from my poem "Draft (September 29, 2016)," which begins with a line by Simone White. "Draft" was previously published online by the *Brooklyn Rail*. Thanks to Simone and to Anselm Berrigan.

Coffee House Press began as a small letterpress operation in 1972 and has grown into an internationally renowned nonprofit publisher of literary fiction, essay, poetry, and other work that doesn't fit neatly into genre categories.

Coffee House is both a publisher and an arts organization. Through our *Books in Action* program and publications, we've become interdisciplinary collaborators and incubators for new work and audience experiences. Our vision for the future is one where a publisher is a catalyst and connector.

LITERATURE
is not the same thing as
PUBLISHING

Coffee House Press is an internationally renowned independent book publisher and arts nonprofit based in Minneapolis, MN; through its literary publications and Books in Action program, Coffee House acts as a catalyst and connector—between authors and readers, ideas and resources, creativity and community, inspiration and action.

Coffee House Press books are made possible through the generous support of grants and donations from corporations, state and federal grant programs, family foundations, and the many individuals who believe in the transformational power of literature. This activity is made possible by the voters of Minnesota through a Minnesota State Arts Board Operating Support grant, thanks to the legislative appropriation from the Arts and Cultural Heritage Fund. Coffee House also receives major operating support from the Amazon Literary Partnership, Jerome Foundation, McKnight Foundation, Target Foundation, and the National Endowment for the Arts (NEA). To find out more about how NEA grants impact individuals and communities, visit www.arts.gov.

Coffee House Press receives additional support from Bookmobile; Dorsey & Whitney LLP; Elmer L. & Eleanor J. Andersen Foundation; Fredrikson & Byron, P.A.; the Matching Grant Program Fund of the Minneapolis Foundation; Mr. Pancks' Fund in memory of Graham Kimpton; the Schwab Charitable Fund; and the U.S. Bank Foundation.

THE PUBLISHER'S CIRCLE OF COFFEE HOUSE PRESS

Publisher's Circle members make significant contributions to Coffee House Press's annual giving campaign. Understanding that a strong financial base is necessary for the press to meet the challenges and opportunities that arise each year, this group plays a crucial part in the success of Coffee House's mission.

Recent Publisher's Circle members include many anonymous donors, Patricia A. Beithon, Anitra Budd, Andrew Brantingham, Dave & Kelli Cloutier, Mary Ebert & Paul Stembler, Jocelyn Hale & Glenn Miller, the Rehael Fund-Roger Hale/Nor Hall of the Minneapolis Foundation, Randy Hartten & Ron Lotz, Dylan Hicks & Nina Hale, William Hardacker, Kenneth & Susan Kahn, Stephen & Isabel Keating, the Kenneth Koch Literary Estate, Cinda Kornblum, Jennifer Kwon Dobbs & Stefan Liess, the Lambert Family Foundation, the Lenfestey Family Foundation, Sarah Lutman & Rob Rudolph, the Carol & Aaron Mack Charitable Fund of the Minneapolis Foundation, Gillian McCain, Malcolm S. McDermid & Katie Windle, Mary & Malcolm McDermid, Daniel N. Smith III & Maureen Millea Smith, Peter Nelson & Jennifer Swenson, Enrique & Jennifer Olivarez, Alan Polsky, Robin Preble, Jeffrey Sugerman & Sarah Schultz, Nan G. Swid, Grant Wood, and Margaret Wurtele.

For more information about the Publisher's Circle and other ways to support Coffee House Press books, authors, and activities, please visit www.coffeehousepress.org/pages/donate or contact us at info@coffeehousepress.org.

ANNA MOSCHOVAKIS is the author of the novel *Eleanor, or, The Rejection of the Progress of Love*, and of three books of poetry, most recently *They and We Will Get Into Trouble for This*. Her translation of David Diop's *At Night All Blood Is Black* (*Frère d'âme*) was awarded the 2020 International Booker Prize. Raised in Los Angeles, she has lived in New York since 1993 and currently makes her home in the Western Catskills.

Participation was designed by
Bookmobile Design & Digital Publisher Services.
Text is set in Adobe Caslon Pro.